K. SEAN HARRIS

I0525922

BLOOD OF
Angels

*A vampire with a craving
for exotic blood travels
to Jamaica ...*

Cover Concept: *K. Sean Harris*
Cover Painting: *Case*
Cover Design: *Sanya Dockery*
Typeset & Book layout: *Sanya Dockery*

Published by: Book Fetish

Printed in the U.S.A   ISBN: 978-976-95303-2-4

NATIONAL LIBRARY OF JAMAICA CATALOGUING-IN-PUBLICATION DATA

Harris, K. Sean
    Blood of angels : a vampire with a craving for exotic blood travels to Jamaica / K. Sean Harris

    p. ; cm.

ISBN 978-976-95303-2-4 (pbk)

1. Jamaican fiction
I. Title

813   dc 22

Only be sure that thou eat not the blood: for the blood is the life; and thou mayest not eat the life with the flesh.

Deuteronomy 12:23

That ye abstain from meats offered to idols, and from blood, and from things strangled, and from fornication: from which if ye keep yourselves, ye shall do well. Fare ye well.

The Acts 15:29

ALSO BY K. SEAN HARRIS:

Novels
- The Kingdom of Death
- The Heart Collector
- Kiss of Death
- The Garrison
- The Stud
- The Stud 11
- Merchants of Death
- Death Incarnate

Anthologies
- Erotic Jamaican Tales
- More Erotic Jamaican Tales
- The Sex Files
- The Sex Files Vol. 2

"Love is the most powerful, most pure aphrodisiac there is."

K. Sean Harris

Chapter 1

Laku felt restless. He was at Showcase, one of the largest nightclubs in Paris, nursing a Remy on the rocks. It was a stunning venue. Superb lighting, large windows with views out to the river, gleaming metalwork, and cool curves in the bar and toilet area. The over one thousand patrons were enjoying DJ Chloe's techno mixes but despite the good vibe, Laku wasn't feeling it. He had gone to the club alone. While in his studio working on his latest project, an abstract piece that he was going to call *Dieu fureur,* God's Fury, he had felt like having a drink and perhaps meet a hot girl to spend the night with. Wouldn't be a bad way to start the weekend.

Two girls had approached him in the hour that he had been there, standing close to the bar, channeling Parisian chic in fitted black denim, wine red Prada boots, a black dress shirt underneath a black and red striped Lacoste cardigan, with a broody look on his face. He wasn't interested in either of them. The blonde had fake breasts, something Laku detested, and the pretty model with the funky hairdo wanted to snort a line of coke off his dick. The latter would have been appealing except that the girl's jealous girlfriend had come over to start an argument.

Drame.

The growing restlessness had now graduated into a sudden urge to leave. He downed the rest of his ridiculously overpriced drink, left the glass on the bar counter and navigated his way through the throng of plastered and pretentious people jumping up and down off beat to Lady Gaga's *Alejandro.* A tall, cute brunette with sparkling green eyes grabbed his ass as he walked by. She licked her lips suggestively when he looked back at her.

She was hot, and clearly drunk, but Laku kept moving, giving in to the weird energy that seemed to be propelling him out of the club. He retrieved his coat and scarf from the coat room and exited the club out into the cold night air.

Franciska, standing across the street, watched as Laku stood in front of the club. She had seen him inside and in a club filled with over four hundred young, virile men, decided that he was the one she wanted to be with tonight. She had focused her mental energy on him, lulling him to come to her. She was as still as a mannequin, except for her flaming red hair, which was dancing in the wind. She ignored the group of four guys that walked by her making lewd comments and laughing hysterically at their own jokes, and watched as he looked around, his eyes finally settling on her. He stared for awhile, a look of confusion and curiosity on his smooth, caramel, handsome face.

He said something to the valet, perhaps letting him know that he wasn't ready for his car, then crossed the street and walked towards her.

She could feel the excitement coursing through her veins as he got closer and closer. Her fangs descended and she slid them back up, as she controlled herself.

She had chosen well.

It was the first time that a human had made her so hungry and horny at the same time.

Chapter 2

" *B*onjour, je suis Laku," Laku said when he got over to the strange woman that seemed to have him hypnotized. When he exited the club he inexplicably felt like he was looking for someone, and when he saw her across the street watching him, he just knew that it was her.

"*Excuses, mais mon francais est terrible.* Do you speak English? Laku. Interesting name," Franciska said, as she took his extended hand, smiling as he flinched involuntarily. "I'm Franciska."

Laku was stunned at how cold her hand was. It was a cold night but her hand felt like it was freezing. Touching her both chilled and warmed him at the same time, making his body tremble slightly in confusion.

"A pleasure to meet you. You are very beautiful." Laku was looking at her intensely. Her heart-shaped face was extremely easy on the eyes. She seemed to be in her mid-twenties. Her large, expressive eyes were mesmerizing. He wasn't sure what colour they were, they appeared to change at whim, making him wonder if he was hallucinating. Her skin was milky white and flawless. She had a generous mouth, with full, inviting lips covered with red lipstick. He imagined kissing them, or having them wrapped around his shaft, sucking him into sweet submission, coaxing his orgasm from deep inside his soul.

He began to have an erection.

"Thank you," she responded, giving him a smile that he could look at for the rest of his life.

Laku cleared his throat and thanked the heavens that he was bundled up in a coat. His erection was raging. He was hornier than he could ever recall being in his twenty-five years. There was something very strange about Franciska but he couldn't put his finger on it. It didn't matter. She didn't make him uncomfortable. Horny, tingly, cold, hot and excited, but there was no discomfort. There was an intense connection between them. One rife with sexual desire but there was something else. There was a feeling of danger that excited him.

He loved her accent. It was European but he wasn't sure which country.

"Where are you from?" he asked, suddenly realizing that they had not released each other's hand since their handshake. He wasn't complaining though. The weird icy hot sensation from her touch was very stimulating.

"Hungary," she told him. "I'm from Benk, a small village, but I live in Budapest now."

"So what are you doing in France? Vacation?"

"The food. I came for the food," Franciska told him wryly. And thus far, she had not been disappointed. The muscular thug that she had devoured last night in Gare du Nord, ironically one of those areas where tourists were advised to avoid, was tasty indeed, though perhaps due to drugs, had left a rather unpleasant aftertaste.

A beautiful, petite woman walking in that area so late at night was supposed to be fair game. The guy had probably thought that it was his birthday to be presented with such a gift. He had wanted money and sex, in that order. She smiled as she remembered the look on his face when she held him by his neck in the air with one hand, toying with him before bringing him down and sinking her fangs into his thick neck, draining every drop of blood from his imposing frame. It was priceless.

Laku smiled at what he perceived to be a joke.

"Did you come alone?"

She raked the middle of his hand with a solitary nail. It sent shivers down his aching groin.

"Yes..."

Laku looked at her for a few moments, his rapid breathing betrayed by the cold air. His breath decorated the air like smoke signals. He knew an invitation when he heard one.

"Let's go back to my place," he said.

"I thought you'd never ask."

Laku felt like he was dreaming. The night had been so surreal. He was used to one night stands but this was different. He had never felt so drawn to someone that he had just met.

They crossed the windswept street, lightly holding hands. Laku noticed the stares from the people outside of the club. It didn't make him uncomfortable as he knew that the stares weren't race related. France, Paris in particular, was quite accommodating towards biracial couples. A handsome black man with a pretty white red-head would only attract attention because of how good they looked together.

Laku wondered if every one could see the sexual energy between them.

It was so palpable, surely it must be visible.

He gestured to the valet to bring his car around.

Two minutes later, they climbed into his black and silver Mini Cooper.

It occurred to Laku as he headed up towards the Pont Alexandre 111, Paris' most beautiful bridge, that tonight felt as though he was acting out a script.

One that was written by Franciska.

He wondered how the rest of it would pan out.

Chapter 3

Laku resided in Ile Saint-Louis, one of the loveliest districts in Paris. Centrally located in the heart of the City of Lights, the island was a visual feast of romantic river banks, eighteenth century houses, refined architecture such as the gilded balconies of the Hotel de Lauzon, specialty shops, art galleries and views of the Seine, which split the isles of Saint-Louis and de la Cite like a beautiful vagina.

Ile Saint-Louis was uniquely calm compared to the rest of Paris, and was a privileged area, home to a mostly upper class older wealthy generation, who usually kept to themselves.

They entered the arched driveway, framed by a sprawling well-manicured lawn. Laku parked and they got out. The ride home had been a quiet one. He had turned the heat on and they listened to Radiohead, while Franciska alternately admired the sights and Laku's side profile.

"You have to invite me in," Franciska said, when Laku opened the elaborate Victorian style front door.

Laku regarded her with a puzzled expression. There was an enigmatic look on her lovely face. Franciska was a strange woman.

"Please, come in," Laku said, bowing slightly as he gestured inside.

"Thank you." Franciska stepped in, smiling at his antics. He was so different. It was as though he had an old soul. She really liked him. A puzzling complication. She was only here to satisfy her lust and thirst. Thoroughly enjoying his company and feeling comfortable in his presence were not supposed to be on the menu.

"Your home is lovely," Franciska said as Laku took her coat, looking around at the high ceiling with century old beams, floor to ceiling windows, wood parquet, antique furniture, the charming marble entertainment center that housed a large flat screen TV. "The past and present co-existing in perfect harmony."

"Thank you," Laku responded as he lit the fireplace. The house had been in his family's possession – his mother's side – for two generations. It had been renovated over the years, but a balance of old world charm and modern necessity had been carefully maintained.

"What do you do?"

Laku poured them a shot of Brandy and handed her a glass.

"I'm an artist," he said, admiring her form beneath the simple black dress. She was petite, but curvy, and had more than her fair share of breasts. They were sitting up in her bra, of which he could see a hint of black lace. His loins stirred. "I paint."

"I see. You must be very good, to be so young and successful."

Laku sipped his drink. He was indeed. He was simply one of the best. But not everyone knew about him, only true collectors and the movers and shakers of the art world were familiar with his incredible talent and work. He was notoriously reclusive and did not do interviews, had in fact turned down an article from Time and a couple of other high profile magazines. He rarely held exhibitions and only had ever done two, one as a student and another a few years later, six months before his parents died. Both collections; ten pieces in the first, and fifteen in the second, had completely sold out in a matter of minutes.

"I am. But all of this is inherited." He gestured with his free hand. "My parents, well my mom, came from wealth. They both died in a car accident two years ago."

"I'm sorry," Franciska said, moving closer to him.

"They were on their way home from a classical concert at the Theatre du Chatelet, when their car skidded on the icy road and slammed into a larger oncoming vehicle. There was an explosion. They died instantly."

Laku downed the rest of his drink in one gulp. Anguish clouded his features. Time had not diminished the loss. The pain was fresh, as though his parents had died yesterday. He was out at Au Chat Noir, a cozy but edgy café having cocktails with Aurore, a photographer he had been seeing at the time, when he heard the news. His father's dear friend, Paul-Henri Moreau, a Brigadier of the Police Nationale, had called him on his mobile.

Laku...J'ai de mauvaises nouvelles. Tes parents sont morts...Je suis desole...

Franciska put her drink down on the coffee table and held his hands. Her touch instantly distracted him from the unpleasant memory. From the phone call that had informed him that he was now an orphan. Her icy hot touch pulled him back to the present, where he had a mysterious Hungarian woman in his living room, the flames from the fireplace illuminating her angelic beauty. She was like a tear from God's eye. Translucent and enchanting. He was intrigued, captivated. He wanted to know her. Wanted her to know him. It wasn't usually like this. He loved to have fun. But when the fun was over he wanted his space. He wasn't into relationships. He already had a woman. He was already in love. He lived and breathed Art. Painting consumed him. Nothing became something. Order from the chaos of his mind.

The orgasmic experience of transforming a blank canvas into a work of art. What woman could compete with that?

Perhaps this one.

He had only known her for two hours and yet he felt more connected to her than he had ever felt to any female, including Gabrielle, the only woman he had been with as a child and as an adult. He lost his virginity to her at fourteen, when she was seventeen, and eleven years later, though she was now married and had a family, they still saw each other every now and then.

Franciska's large expressive eyes, which seemed inexplicably to be a different colour every time Laku looked into them – they were now a grayish green – stared up at him intensely. Her eyes were captivating pools filled with emotions that Laku couldn't read, couldn't understand, save one. Lust. Her passion and desire for him excited and scared him at the same time.

Everything about her seemed to affect him in twos. Dual emotions that contradicted each other and placed him in a heightened state of awareness. He could feel the heat radiating from her cold body. He could hear her melodic breathing, the cackle of the burning wood in the fireplace, the sound of his own heart pounding desperately, like he was doing laps in the *Tour de France*. The almost painful throbbing of his erect member, as it cried for freedom from the confines of his jeans.

Franciska glided into his arms and pulled his head down to hers before Laku even realized that she had moved.

Time was nonexistent as their lips inched towards each other for what seemed like an eternity, the gap finally bridged as their lips became one. The kiss was slow, soft, gentle and sweet. Franciska slipped her tongue inside Laku's mouth, exploring, seeking, and finding, the exquisite pleasures that were hers for the taking.

Laku moaned. A low primal sound that increased the moisture between Franciska's legs. She intensified her kiss, their tongues doing a frenzied waltz as she pressed her supple body against his forcefully, his erection boring a hole in her stomach, as he gripped her ass cheeks and caressed them through the silky fabric of her dress.

Laku was breathless when she broke the kiss.

Franciska, her eyes now as red as her flaming hair, unbuckled his jeans and slipped them to his ankles. She then pulled down his black boxer-briefs. His dick sprang free like an angry cobra. Franciska purred as she squatted in front of him and caressed it gently with her cold, soft hands. The icy hot sensation of her touch was manifested twofold on his shaft. The feeling was indescribable. His member throbbed in her grasp, confused at being cold and hot at the same time.

Laku grunted audibly when she took him inside her mouth. His knees threatened to give way as she slowly swallowed him all the way in, his scrotum resting against the dimple in her chin. Her tongue seemed to caress every bulging vein as she slid his member in and out of her mouth, deep-throating him effortlessly despite his formidable size.

"Franciska...*Ca sent trop bon...doux Jésus*," Laku groaned, reverting to his native tongue as pleasure held him in a vice grip and threatened to make him climax before he was ready.

Franciska's tongue was wrapped around his pulsing shaft like a velvet snake as she sucked him relentlessly, ravenously.

Laku's teeth were tightly clenched and his knees wobbled as he fought valiantly to delay his climax.

He lost.

"*Oh mon Dieu! Je viens!*" Laku shouted as he climaxed down her willing throat, trembling furiously from the intensity of his orgasm.

Franciska swallowed every drop.

Chapter 4

Laku stumbled over to the antique sofa and plopped down breathlessly, his knees no longer able to support his one hundred and eighty-four pound frame. He watched Franciska through narrowed slits, his chest heaving mightily, as she crawled towards him, her impossibly red eyes blazing passionately.

Laku wondered if he was delirious. It simply was not possible for her eyes to be so red. Fear, coupled with a passion so intense he had trouble catching his breath, took a hold of him. A part of him wanted to get away from her, and a part of him wanted to be inside her. He couldn't move to obey either voice. His limbs were not cooperating with his brain.

He sat there immobile, with the exception of his heaving chest, and watched as she removed his boots, his socks, his boxers and his jeans. She then stood and undressed, slipping off her silky black dress, revealing matching black lace underwear.

She removed her bra, displaying perfectly proportioned breasts, which were obviously immune to gravity. Her nipples were a bright pink, and they pointed at Laku accusingly, blaming him for their current state.

Laku felt like he was having an out of body experience. His senses were acutely sharpened and he was feeling indescribable sensations coursing through his body, yet he was unable to move. He could not speak, or move his hands and legs. His shaft had no such trouble. It was waving like an iron flag, still rock hard and throbbing, despite having just experienced the most intense orgasm of his life.

She slid off her panties and touched herself, spreading her glistening pink folds as she toyed with her clitoris, which was as hard as granite. She was a natural red-head, as the neatly trimmed triangular patch of red hair above her vagina indicated. She maintained eye contact with Laku as she brought herself to a climax, her juices lubricating her fingers and staining her thighs as she moaned in ecstasy.

Despite staring at her the entire time, Laku didn't see when she moved but Franciska was now suddenly on top of him, his shaft buried inside her hot depths. Her pussy felt like a vise filled with warm flowing honey. She clutched him by the throat and moaned his name as she bounced up and down in a frenzy, impaling herself mercilessly over and over again.

Laku felt like a male blow-up doll as he soaked in the incredible sensations assaulting his body via his member, though he was still unable to move. She was grinding on his dick so forcefully he feared that she was going to break it off inside her. He wished that he could move so he could give as good as he was getting, but his scary and mind boggling paralysis was still in effect.

He could feel her tight wetness contracting as she convulsed and her sugar walls caved in on his shaft.

She was coming.

Hard.

Franciska wavered between killing Laku and intensifying her orgasm for several seconds as her climax rippled through her frame, her fangs bared, her head thrown back aloft as she struggled to control herself. She had to dig deep down to find the restraint but she did. Her screams, which sounded like a blend of frustration and sheer ecstasy, reverberated throughout the expansive house.

She slumped against Laku, freeing him as she shivered and moaned in his arms.

"Basszus...basszus...basszus..."

Laku was immediately aware that he could now move and he hugged her tightly, wondering what she was whispering. Wondering what in heaven's name had just transpired. Franciska had shaken so hard during her lengthy orgasm that the entire couch had rattled.

He felt like he had returned from a far away place. He was shaking too. Relief washed over him though he had no idea what he was relieved about. This wasn't sex. He simply couldn't find the word to describe their coupling. It was out of this world.

"*Átkozott...*"

He kept hugging her and stroking her curly untamed mane. Incredibly, he was still rock hard inside her.

Franciska's shaking finally subsided and she rocked back, purring at the feel of the caramel steel deeply embedded inside her as she adjusted herself.

She placed her hands on either side of his face and looked at him. Why hadn't she killed him? That was the plan. Great sex and the drinking of his blood as she climaxed. The sex wasn't just great, it had been phenomenal. She could only imagine how incredible her orgasm would have been had she indulged. He smelled so good. Tasted even better. So good in fact that she had climaxed from giving him fellatio. That had never happened to her before, definitely not with Rikard, her maker.

It had taken every ounce of willpower in her being not to suck the life out of Laku's gorgeous body. And gorgeous it was. Six feet of succulent caramel chocolate goodness. Broad shoulders; wide chest; flat stomach; a defined V that led to his generously endowed genitalia; strong, robust legs; sculpted arms and a face that was almost too pretty for a man to have. Aristocratic nose, high cheekbones, bushy eyebrows, light brown eyes, soft kissable lips anchored by a strong chin, smooth caramel skin, Laku was indeed a fine specimen.

She uttered a feline moan as she felt him throb inside her.

She sighed as she caressed his face.

She couldn't kill him.

It would be a waste.

Besides, it was clear that she was quickly developing an attachment to him.

That was not good. But what to do? She would think about it later. Right now she wanted, no needed, him to fuck her into eternity.

She got off his lap and sank to the carpet on her hands and knees. Laku groaned at the exquisite rear view of her glistening sex.

She turned her head and fixed him with a carnal gaze.

"*Baszd meg Laku...*"

Laku didn't speak Hungarian but he knew exactly what that meant.

He stooped over her and entered her with a firm thrust.

Franciska emitted a rather unfeminine grunt.

Laku, now free to fuck her with wild abandon, wasted no time in getting down to business. He gripped a fistful of her mane as he stroked her with purpose, going deep and hard, relishing the feel of her slippery succulent heat.

"Oh Laku...*Baszd meg!*"

Laku quickened his pace, growling like a provoked lion as he pounded Franciska viciously, extracting another orgasm from her by force, making her howl his name as she ripped the carpet apart with her bare hands.

"Laku! Laku! Laku! *Jövök! Jövök!*" Franciska roared. Her body felt like it had exploded into a million atoms of pleasure.

Laku was mere seconds behind. He could feel his orgasm surging towards his center, his body anxiously urging it on, ready for sweet release. Ready for its nirvana.

He looked up as he climaxed with an intensity that rattled his soul.

His eyes bulged in fear and confusion as he spilled his hot seed forcefully inside Franciska's depths.

He was looking in the mirror above the fireplace.

All he could see was his own reflection.

Chapter 5

Laku opened his eyes. He was disoriented. He was lying on the carpet. He was nude. He laid there for a few moments, until the fog in his head started to clear. It was all coming back to him now. Last night. Franciska. Her peculiar, intoxicating presence. His strange paralysis. The animalistic, primal, no holds barred coupling. The indescribable sensations. The gut-wrenching fear and confusion that had gripped him when he looked in the mirror at his most vulnerable moment, as his seed anxiously left his body in a rush of intense pleasure, and did not see Franciska's reflection.

That was the extent of his recollection. As hard as he tried, he could remember nothing beyond that point. He wondered what time it was. The windows were shut and the drapes were tightly pulled. He rose and walked unsteadily over to the nearest window, his shaft, stained with Franciska's juices, swinging like a pendulum. His head felt light, like he would faint any minute now.

He opened the drapes a bit and looked out through the glass window. This window, at the right side of the living room, gave him a partial view of the quiet street that his house was on. It was a dreary day. Cold, bleak and gray.

Laku turned away and walked over to the coffee table. He picked up the glass that Franciska had drunk out of. There was red lipstick where her soft lips had massaged the rim of the glass as she drank. There was still some brandy left in the glass. Laku looked down on the carpet where he had roughly taken her from behind and his eyes bulged with disbelief. The rug was ruined. Tufts of the thick expensive rug had been ripped out, exposing the parquet flooring.

Laku looked at the damage in amazement. How the hell had that happened? He sat down on the sofa and stared at the fireplace. The fire was just about dying; having been burning since 2:30 a.m. Laku had been taught an extremely effective method of building a fire. It was called an upside-down fire. You started with a substantial amount of very dry wood, putting the largest logs at the bottom, tightly packed with no space between them. The process was repeated with each layer of log smaller than the last. At the top you placed crumpled paper or fire-starter oil sticks. There was no backdraft smoke in the house and it burned beautifully unattended for up to seven hours depending on the amount and type of wood used.

It was now 8:00 a.m., according to the handsome antique grandfather clock on the wall between two paintings, one of his father and the other of his mother. He had done them when he was only sixteen. Both paintings showcased his masterful use of light and shadow, and were very eloquent odes to his parents. A family friend, a wealthy art collector, saw them on a visit once and offered two hundred and eighty thousand Euros each for the two paintings.

He was flatly refused. They were a deeply personal work and up to that point, Laku's most impressive demonstration of his prodigious talent.

Laku forced himself to confront what he had not seen in the mirror. He had been inside of Franciska, and she was in front of him, screaming her head off, thrashing in primal ecstasy as he pummeled her with unbridled lust, yet he had only seen his own reflection.

Every true artist was crazy, some a little, others a lot. Insanity and intelligence were after all, first cousins. But he was not mad. That much he was sure of. Rather eccentric, very broody, viewed the world in high definition, but quite sane. Having satisfied himself of his mental state, he tried to find a logical explanation. Surely there had to be one. There had to be a reasonable explanation for how a woman could make him paralyzed during sex, could have the strength to rip holes in a thick rug with her bare hands, to be cold and hot at the same time, and to somehow cannot be seen through a mirror.

Then there was the little matter of his inability to remember anything after the mirror episode. Several theories assaulted his brain. He rejected them, except for one. But it was impossible. Or was it? An avid reader of just about everything, he had read books about them and found them mildly interesting, if nothing else. But several of the so-called myths and characteristics were stuck in his head. Franciska's unnatural paleness. Her cold skin. Her unusual eyes. Her speed. Her strength. Her general *weirdness.* Her reflection unable to be seen in a mirror.

Il ne pouvait pas être!

Laku rubbed his temple. His head was beginning to throb. Partly because of hunger, but mostly because his imagination was trying to convince him that Franciska was a vampire.

It was succeeding.

You have to invite me in.

It was said that vampires cannot enter someone's home unless invited.

Why did you come to France?

For the food. I came for the food.

The more he thought about it, the more he was convinced.

Laku wasn't sure what was scarier. The fact that he had been with a vampire and had surely hovered between life and death throughout the course of the night, or the fact that he was excited, amazed, enthralled and desperately wanted to see her again.

Perhaps he was insane after all.

After breakfast at Le Flores en Ile, one of the two cafés in Ile de St. Louis overlooking the Pont Marie, where he had beignets, chausson aux pommes, and coffee, Laku went home to paint. He was inspired. He had to recapture his experience last night. Interpret it artistically. Immortalize it on canvas.

His art studio was at the back of the house. It was large, airy and neat, apart from the immediate work area, which was in the middle of the room. It had one ceiling to floor window that Laku usually kept open, night or day, as long as he was working. But it was closed now. With Christmas only three weeks away, Paris was cold and windy.

A large enclosed cupboard that was divided in two, and had a breathtaking painting of Laku's interpretation of The Last Supper on the sliding door, stayed shut and housed everything that was not in current use. Four of Laku's paintings adorned the wall facing the entrance to the studio.

Attired in a pair of ripped, distressed jeans underneath a white coat, Laku attacked the canvas like a man possessed. He didn't have to think. Inspiration flowed from the dark recesses of his mind as imagination and actual experience manifested on the canvas with an ethereal brilliance.

He was relentless in his efforts, stopping only to use the bathroom.

At ten p.m. he stopped abruptly. It was as though an internal timer had sounded that he was finished.

He was thoroughly exhausted.

He felt utterly exhilarated.

He stepped back and viewed the painting.

It literally took his breath away.

It was the most disturbingly beautiful thing he had ever seen.

Chapter 6

Franciska watched Laku as he slept. He was clad in dark blue boxer-briefs, lying on his stomach in the large four poster antique bed. He was dead to the world. She had entered the house a few minutes past midnight. She had waited until he was asleep.

Laku had been on her mind from the moment she left the house after rendering him unconscious. When Laku climaxed she had felt a change in his energy and had looked back to see his face frozen in shock, ecstasy and fear, as he looked in the mirror above the fireplace.

She knew that he had realized that she was not human.

She should have killed him then, but she didn't. Instead she had made him unconscious, and against her better judgement, left him lying naked on the carpeted floor. She wasn't sure what to make of his reaction to his discovery. He seemed fascinated. Intrigued. Excited. Any initial fear that he might have felt was gone. He wanted to see her again. She couldn't read his mind but she could feel his energy. That was how she was able to re-enter the house without him inviting her in again. She was more than welcome.

Keeping track of his movements mentally, she knew that he had briefly left the house to have breakfast before heading back home to paint.

He had recreated that pivotal moment when he made his discovery. When she entered the house, she had headed straight to the studio to look at the painting.

She was no art connoisseur but even someone with cataracts could see that it was a phenomenal piece of work.

He had captured every detail, every nuance. It was erotic, sensual, and disturbing, eerie even.

The painting looked *alive.*

It had the odor of love. She could *smell* it. Laku was in love with her. Fascinating. How could a man, especially one as sophisticated and wealthy such as Laku, fall in love with something that was undead? She knew that she was beautiful, but surely her outer beauty could not be enough for him to disregard the fact that she was a predator, a killer. He should be repulsed, sickened, and scared for his life. And his soul.

But he wasn't.

Franciska sighed.

Falling for this handsome, virile man was not in the cards. There was no room for that in her life. The complications of being with a human aside, there was the little matter of Rikard, her maker. He would destroy her and kill Laku, before he let her go.

She had to end this before it got any further.

There was no future for them.

Nothing.

She had to kill him.

She climbed on top of his sleeping form and lowered her mouth to his neck.

Her fangs descended with an audible click.

Rikard drew harshly on the cigarette. He was smoking Sopiane, a local brand. Rikard was a smoker before he became a vampire and a hundred and fifteen years later, he had yet to kick the habit. He enjoyed it and besides, it wasn't like he had to worry about getting lung cancer. There was nothing like a smoke after a good meal. He flicked the accumulated ash on the life-less body next to him.

He was in an alley beside a seedy strip club on Vaci utca, one of the most popular thoroughfares in central Budapest. The dead man, an unlucky tourist from England, had gotten into a fight with a patron and was thrown out of the club. His three friends, drunk and having a good time, decided that they would stay and catch up with him later at the hotel.

Rikard had pounced as the man wiped the blood from his busted lip, hurling drunken racial slurs to no one in particular. The bouncers had gone back inside after tossing him into the street. He had quickly snatched him and taken him into the alley.

Fear had sobered the man immediately.

It was the last emotion he had felt.

Rikard had sucked the life out of his thrashing body, drinking his warm blood until there was nothing left. It was his second victim of the night. He was now sated. He would go home soon.

Rikard was slightly troubled. His mind was on Franciska. She had taken trips without him a few times before and it had never been a problem, but this one was different. He was feeling a strange vibe whenever he tuned into her energy. She felt distracted. Preoccupied. Distant. Which had nothing to do with the distance. He didn't like it.

He had convinced himself that Franciska loved him, how much, he wasn't sure. What he was sure of was that she was loyal to him as her maker, and that she feared him. That was enough for him. Franciska was the kind of woman he would never have been able to get under normal circumstances. But he had saved her life, and given her a new life. She was forever in his debt, and he liked it that way. Franciska. His beautiful treasure. She would always be his.

He put the cigarette out, using the man's eyeball as an ashtray.

She was due back in another week or so.

If the vibe intensified before then, he would go to Paris.

Chapter 7

L aku opened his eyes suddenly. His dream had felt so real. Then he felt Franciska on top of him, her cold, razor-sharp teeth on his flesh. He abruptly realized that his dream was real.

"Do it," Laku whispered. He couldn't stop her anyway and he really wanted to see if what she was feeling for him wasn't enough to stop her from turning him into a late night snack. Strangely, he felt no fear as his life hung in the balance. There was a hollow feeling in his stomach and a throbbing pain in his heart, induced by the fact that she might not care enough about him not to kill him. He feared that, more than death itself.

Breathing heavily, Franciska flew from off Laku and leaned against the bedroom wall. She was shaking uncontrollably. She couldn't do it. She knew that she should, but she couldn't. It was impossible for her to take his life. She was in love with a human. That he could fall for her knowing what she was endeared him even more to her.

Laku turned around to look at her. His heart was beating so fast he feared that he would go into cardiac arrest. They stared at each other in the softly lit room, bathed by the full moon that was visible through the entire east wall, which was made of glass.

Laku got up and walked over to her slowly. He felt like he was floating on air. His heart was smiling. She loved him. If she didn't, he would now be dead and his pristine white sheets would be stained with his blood.

He stood close to her and cupped her face. She was crying. Tears of blood flowed down her pale white cheeks. Love was an involuntary emotion. And it remained an emotion until one turned it into an action. Laku kissed her forehead; then he claimed her shivering lips.

Franciska cried as she ardently returned his kiss. How was it possible for her to love this human so much? She had been Rikard's partner for twenty years and had only known Laku for two days, yet her love for him was a bottomless abyss, echoing with emotions and sensations that she had never felt as a human, or as a vampire. It was inexplicable. It was real. It was sweet torment. Sadistic love. She was putting him in grave danger by loving him. But she could not help herself. She had fallen hard in love, and getting up was impossible.

Laku opened her coat. She was naked underneath. He devoured her breasts, sucking them and biting her nipples with restrained force, making Franciska moan and utter words that he did not understand.

He slid to his knees and breathed in her essence.

He held her by her ass cheeks as he buried his face inside her love, licking and sucking her sweet nectar ravenously, his nose brushing forcefully against her clit, making her toes curl in the confines of her black boots.

"*Igen! Igen! Igen!*

Laku pursed his lips and sucked on her clit insistently.

"*Jövök! Jövök!*"

Franciska, bloody tears streaking down her cheeks and dripping on top of Laku's head, vibrated in his knowledgeable mouth, her knees turning to jelly, as she climaxed.

"Oh Laku...*te vagy a legjobb...*"

Laku raised his head finally, and stood.

He scooped her in his arms in one fluid motion, and took her to his bed.

He removed her coat and her boots, and swiftly discarded his underwear.

"*Szeretlek...*" Franciska whispered, as she planted tiny kisses all over his face.

Laku didn't understand the word but the look in her eyes translated it.

"*Je t'aime trop,*" Laku responded, before devouring her mouth and slipping deep inside her wetness.

Franciska groaned and wrapped her legs around him tightly, locking him inside her erotic embrace.

Laku had just escaped death.

Now he was certain that he was going to die from pleasure.

Chapter 8

Franciska sighed contentedly in Laku's arms. Her cheeks were uncharacteristically rosy, courtesy of the four intense orgasms that Laku had wrenched from her. So this was what love felt like. It was a totally exhilarating feeling. There was no place in the world that she would rather be, than where she was at that moment. Lying in Laku's arms, in his bed, basking in the afterglow of their magical sex, was a memory that would forever be a part of her consciousness.

But it was all an illusion. There was no future for them. Laku was a special human, so that wasn't the problem. The problem was Rikard. He would never release her to be with someone else.

She remembered that hot summer in Budapest twenty years ago like it was yesterday. She was twenty-six years old then, three years had passed since she left

Benk, the small village where she had been born and raised, for the brighter lights of Budapest, the capital of Hungary. Back then Hungary was a Soviet satellite, one of the less hard-line regimes of Eastern Europe but Communist nevertheless.

With her beautiful looks, she had scored several gigs modeling lingerie and was a sales representative in a luxury goods store, living in a small flat in central Budapest. She had disembarked the train and was walking home one Friday evening at 6 p.m. when she was kidnapped and thrown into a vehicle by three men, a spurned admirer and two of his friends. She was taken to a filthy abandoned warehouse and brutally raped by all three men. She was also beaten to a pulp, stabbed and left for dead.

Rikard had found her, near dead from the loss of the blood. Even in her violated state, she had stirred something in him, and he had saved her by giving her some of his vampire blood to drink. He turned her into a vampire, changing her life forever. She got her revenge against the three men that had violated her so savagely. One of them had inadvertently dropped his wallet and left it at the scene. She tracked him down and after getting the information on where to find the other two men, had beaten him, sucked him dry and ripped his head from his body. The rest suffered a similar fate.

The local police had attributed the grotesque killings to gang violence.

Laku was toying with her hair, studying her face in the soft light as though he had never seen her before. Franciska smiled at him. He was so handsome, almost too pretty for a man. He was like a perfectly sculpted bronzed statue. Surely he must know the magnitude of his appeal but he was unaffected by it. Rikard was nothing like Laku. The only thing they had in common was that they were both tall.

Rikard was very skinny, almost emaciated, with long blonde hair and hawk-like features. He had never told her how he became a vampire but she knew that he used to be a blacksmith before he became one. He was very fond of his 'beautiful treasure' as he sometimes referred to her. He never used to let her out of his sight but with time, came a reluctant trust, and he didn't mind her solo feeding trips as long as she didn't stay too long. He was ill-tempered, and often over-bearing.

She didn't love him, and never would, even if they were together for another two hundred years. And he knew that, but she knew he would never let her go.

She kissed Laku's forehead. She knew that he had a lot of questions to ask her, and she marveled at his restraint. Anyone else would have been babbling, anxious to know if everything that they had heard about vampires were true.

She wouldn't wait for him to ask, she would tell him. He also needed to know that his life would be in danger, if it wasn't already. Surely Rikard had sensed the shift in her energy by now. And as her feelings for Laku engulfed her more and more, he would sense that something was wrong. He didn't have the power to read her mind, but when she was in his presence, he could see whatever she sees, or has seen, if he held her head in his hands and focused on her eyes. He would see everything that had taken place in Paris, if he decided to look. Then all hell would break loose. Rikard had a terrible temper and he was very jealous of her.

Franciska sighed.

She snuggled up even closer to Laku, and as they stared into each other's eyes, she told him everything.

Chapter 9

"Why don't you leave him?" Laku asked, breaking the silence after Franciska's long talk. He had listened keenly and had not interrupted her even once.

"I can't. The penalty for a vampire leaving his or her maker without permission is death. He would kill me. He is much stronger and more powerful than I am. He would destroy me Laku. And you..."

Laku hated the hold this Rikard had over the woman that he loved. It was a hold that he had to break. He could not allow Franciska to go back to Hungary. He would not allow it. She had to stay here with him.

"I'm not letting you go back," Laku said quietly but firmly.

Franciska could *feel* the passion in his words.

"I have to go back Laku. I would never forgive myself if I allowed something to happen to you."

"Turn me into a vampire. Then I'll be able to protect us." He sat up and pulled her up. "That is our only chance to be together."

Tears streamed down Franciska's cheeks for the second time that night. Did Laku really know what he was asking her to do? Did he think that it was an easy life being a vampire? Hell it wasn't even a life. It was a lonely, secret existence. They were undead. Vile creatures. Some more vile than others. Hunters and predators. And though she was sure that due to Laku's innate genius he would have extraordinary powers if he were to become a vampire, and he would be very strong as a newborn, it wasn't a certainty that he would be able to defeat Rikard.

Rikard was part of a coven of seven vampires. He would enlist their help if he needed to. There was no way Laku could defeat them all, even with her help. It was hopeless.

She said as much to Laku.

"Just do it," was his reply.

Franciska was amazed that he would do that just for a chance to be with her.

It overwhelmed her. She started crying again. She had lost so much blood crying that she was hungry. She would need to feed soon. Now was as good a time as any. Give Laku time to think. Though deep down she knew that he meant what he said and would not change his mind.

She got up and got dressed abruptly.

Laku watched her with questioning eyes.

"I'll be back before daybreak. I promise."

And with that she was gone.

Laku got up, slipped on a black Yves Saint Laurent robe and padded out to the mini bar in the living room. He poured a drink from his €4,000 bottle of vintage Romanee Costi and sat on the love seat in front of the fireplace. He swirled his glass for several seconds, inhaled the aroma of the wine and took a sip. The wine was like velvet to his palate. It warmed his body and soothed his troubled soul.

Fantasy was now his reality. They had collided violently, leaving an emotional wreck that he was now trying to sift through. In two days his world had been turned upside down. He recounted the facts. Vampires were real. He had fallen deeply in love with one of them. She was also in love with him. His life and her existence were now in danger because of this love. Her maker, Rikard, the vampire who turned her into one, would destroy her and kill him if he found out about their unholy love. Laku felt like he was a character in a novel. How crazy could life get? If the events of the past two days were anything to go by, crazy beyond anything he could have ever imagined, and he always thought that he was very imaginative.

He looked up at the portraits of his parents. He wondered what they would think. He doubted his dad would have understood. His mom had been a free-spirited, adventurous woman; after all she married his father, an Egyptian, against her snobby wealthy parents' wishes and despite their threats to cut her out of the will. Yes. His mother had been a rebellious romantic. She would have gotten it.

He finished the wine and savoured the after taste. The flavour impression lingered long after his last swallow. Reminded him of Franciska's peach.

Franciska.

She had permeated his mind, body and soul.

How could she expect him to live without her?

She had to do as he asked.

The alternative was unthinkable.

Chapter 10

Franciska returned two and a half hours later. Laku was still sitting in the living room, thinking and waiting for her. She hugged him from behind and kissed him softly on the neck. She marveled inwardly at the power of love. She had never seen anyone whose blood she wanted to drink so badly, yet she was able to restrain herself because she loved him.

Laku reached up to run his fingers through her hair with one hand.

"Let's go for a walk. Is it ok for you to watch the sunrise?"

Franciska chuckled.

"Yes, I won't just combust if sunlight catches me like you see in the movies or read in some books. Being in the sun will weaken me mentally and physically, but unless I'm directly exposed to it continuously for a lengthy period, it won't be fatal."

"That's great. Watching the sunrise by the Seine is one of the most beautiful sights there is," Laku told her. He got up and they went inside his bedroom.

"You're very talented," Franciska remarked, as they strolled arm in arm up the street. They were both dressed in full black. Laku was wearing rugged Ferragamo boots, jeans, sweater and a double-breasted Vuitton tweed coat. The only thing that Franciska was wearing that belonged to her was her knee high boots and underwear. Laku, knowing that he would go to a café for breakfast before returning home, was mindful to ensure that she would be adequately covered if it turned out to be a bright sunny morning. She was dressed in one of Laku's sweaters and a hooded trench coat. A pair of sunglasses and a pair of gloves were in the coat pocket.

"Thanks, an artistic genius they say," Laku responded. Franciska knew that he was being truthful and not boastful. Laku was very unpretentious despite his wealth and immense talent. "That painting of us, *épiphanie magique,* is one of my most prized possessions. I'll never be able to create something like that again. The inspiration I received that day was one of a kind."

"The name you gave it…what does that mean?"

Laku stopped and crushed her to him, kissing her deeply before responding.

"Magical epiphany."

Franciska smiled. "I like it."

They continued their stroll to the Pont Alexandre 111 Bridge in the frigid morning air, which was approximately six blocks from Laku's home.

Their timing was perfect. Laku stood behind her and hugged her to him. Other people were close by, but at that moment they were alone in the universe. They watched in awe as the sky turned pink and yellow while the sun rose above the splendid river, caressing the water and the monuments as it ascended.

C'etait magnifique.

Franciska almost felt human.

Laku brought out the best in her. The emotions of a vampire were far stronger than that of a human. And being around Laku, basking in his enlightening love, and looking at the most romantic city in the world through the starry eyes of a lover, made her feel emotions with an intensity that was as powerful as it was startling. It was unlike anything that she had ever felt before.

It was nothing short of cruel, for the stars to align like this, suddenly giving her Laku, letting her experience what real love was like, blessing her with the experience of a lifetime, only for it to be taken away just as quickly.

She would not do as Laku asked. She would not put him in harm's way. They were already flirting with danger. They would have to accept their fate. Embrace their destiny. They could not be together regardless of the love that they shared.

At least she would always have these wonderful memories, though it would not fill the vacuum in her soulless body.

Laku gave her a brief history of the bridge, which was a marvel of nineteenth century engineering, and the monuments that featured prominently in the bridge. Franciska especially admired the charming, playful statue of a nymph riding a fish.

They strolled along rue de St. Louis en Ile, the main street, window-shopping at the numerous wonderful boutique and specialty shops. Most of the places were closed, as it was still quite early, but one of the small take-out cafés was open, and Laku purchased coffee, bagels, cheese and fruit to take home.

He sipped his coffee as they slowly made their way home. He doubted he had ever been happier in his life than he was now. And that was frightening. He had lived a blessed and happy life, filled with love, care, passion and wealth. Yet nothing compared to the joy that he felt when he was with Franciska.

"Do you love him?"

Franciska shook her head. "No," she said simply. "Never had, never will."

Laku thought that was the saddest thing he had ever heard. He couldn't imagine being with someone for twenty years that he didn't love yet couldn't leave.

"You're not going back," Laku said forcefully.

Franciska didn't respond.

She didn't know who it was going to hurt more when she went back to Hungary, him or her.

It was going to be the hardest thing that she would ever have to do in her existence.

But she had to find the strength to do it.

She had no choice, not if she wanted Laku to live.

They were silent, both tightly wrapped inside their own thoughts, for the rest of the journey.

Chapter 11

The following twelve days were a romantic blur of ridiculously hot sex, long romantic late-night walks along the Seine, clubbing – vampires were not affected by artificial light, long talks by the fireplace drinking expensive vintage wine and sight seeing. They spent every minute of every day together. Even when Laku painted, as Franciska urged him to do as she wanted to watch him create his masterpieces, she was right there, marveling at his skill, and she was as excited as he was when he finished *Dieu fureur*, the piece that he had been working on when he met her.

On Friday night, exactly two weeks to the day that they entered each other's lives, Franciska knew that it was time. She couldn't wait any longer. Her gut feeling was telling her that time was running out. The honeymoon was over. She was so totally immersed in Laku that there was no question that Rikard must be feeling the severe disconnect whenever he tapped into her energy. He would be worried and angry, and if she didn't return now, he would come looking for her. And eventually, he would find her. She didn't want to think about what would happen then.

She looked at Laku's sleeping form for a long time, as though she was committing every detail to memory. The confusing but beautiful abstract tattoo that covered his entire back. His smooth caramel skin. His broad shoulders. His soft, curly hair. His sculpted cheekbones. She wondered what he was dreaming about. She wished that she had the power to read his thoughts. He looked so peaceful. So serene. The fact that she was about to shatter that serenity and break his heart, and hers in the process, made her contemplate jumping headfirst into the fireplace and burn herself slowly and painfully out of this world. She was certain that it would be less painful than what she was about to do.

"Viszlat szerelmem." She planted a soft kiss on his cheek. He stirred but didn't awaken.

She couldn't believe that this was the last time she would be seeing him. The pain in her heart was excruciating, like someone had driven a wooden stake through it. How could a heart that does not beat be filled with so much wretched pain? How could an undead being feel so *alive?*

She had to go before she became weak and changed her mind. She was about to turn away when something hit her.

If Rikard did indeed come to Paris, or was already here, he would still end up at Laku's home even if she left now. And he would still kill Laku whether she was here or not.

Nem!

She could not take the chance and leave Laku defenseless. She would never forgive herself. She would have to turn him into a vampire, leave for Hungary immediately, and keep her fingers crossed that Rikard was still there; and she would catch him before he came to Paris.

This was not an easy decision for her.

This was not a life she would have chosen for herself; much less to give it to someone that she loved more than anything in this world.

But it was the only way.

"Sajnalom szerelmem."

Fangs bared, she gently lifted his head from off the pillow and pierced his virgin neck.

Laku woke up to pain that was so excruciating he wished that he was dead.

His agonizing screams saved his life. Franciska was almost unable to stop. His blood, so rich and sweet, and pure, which she had desired for so long, transformed her into the predator that she really was, and she got lost in the moment, gorging uncontrollably until his blood-curling screams pulled her back from the edge.

Panting, her large beautiful eyes blazing red in an intricate blend of excitement and horror, she released him abruptly and flew backwards from off of the bed.

Laku's blood had stained her lips, teeth and chin like a blind woman had haphazardly applied red lipstick to her mouth.

She had almost killed him.

She shuddered at the thought.

She looked at his frame writhing on the bed in pure agony. Franciska was stunned. It was the fastest transformation she had ever seen. Based on the level of his excruciating pain, the venom was already, incredibly, rapidly circulating through his blood stream. Usually the changing process was slow. Transformation usually took three to five days. At this rate, it would take less than half a day for the venom to saturate every cell in his body. Laku was even more special than she had realized. She could only imagine how powerful he would be once the process was complete. Usually newborns were uncontrollable, and without an older vampire to guide and lead them, they tended to draw dangerous attention to themselves, killing at will and alarming the humans.

That in turn would attract the unwanted attention of *Die Auserwählten,* the Chosen Ones. Powerful and ancient, having been in existence for over four thousand years, they were the acknowledged vampire authority. They were from the Black Forest region in Germany, and they made their presence felt whenever renegade vampires went too far in their activities. They would kill troublesome newborns, as well as the vampires who created them.

But she suspected that even without supervision, Laku would not be a typical newborn. She sure hoped so, for his and all their sakes. If he caught the attention of the Chosen Ones, they would kill him, her, and the entire coven that she was associated with. She didn't care about the lives of Rikard and the others, not even hers, not after this, but she didn't want anything to happen to Laku.

Laku was looking at her now, his handsome face showing the effects of the wretched pain that he was enduring. Pain, anguish and confusion shone in his eyes. She could see the love too. He reached out to her. Franciska couldn't take it anymore. She wanted to comfort him, hold him, be there for him, let him know that it would soon be over.

Franciska fled.

Chapter 12

"*Kurva!*" Rikard thundered, as he administered a vicious backhanded slap to Franciska's face, sending her crashing into the wall a few feet away. She had arrived back in Hungary less than half an hour ago, and had headed straight home. The coven was a large house in Buda Hills, in District 12. Old but charming, and shrouded by lots of trees, the house used to be owned by an eccentric retired doctor, who had lived there alone.

He was killed by Domonkos, one of the seven vampires that now lived there along with Rikard and Franciska, several years ago when he stumbled upon the house while hunting prey. Domonkos took control of the house and over the years, had invited other vampires that he was cool with to form a coven. They all guarded the territory together from other vampires and sometimes hunted together.

Domonkos and Rikard were the two most powerful vampires in the coven. Covens rarely lasted long. Fights about supremacy and conformity tended to break them up after a while. This one had been around for ten years, a short space of time in the ageless life of vampires.

They were in their room. Rikard had immediately assaulted her with a barrage of questions about her trip to Paris. Not satisfied with her responses, he had gripped her face painfully and stared into her eyes, extracting what she wouldn't tell him. He saw flashes of her adventure in Paris.

He saw her coupling with an extraordinarily handsome man, fucking him with wild abandon, blissfully screaming his name in ecstasy. She had never been so naturally passionate with him. In one frame he saw a look on her face that made him physically recoil. She was hugging the same man, watching the sunset, her beautiful face sporting an expression that was unmistakably that of a woman in love. That had thrown him into a blind rage.

The wall cracked from Franciska's impact. The heavy moosehead hanging on the wall fell on top of her, as she lay on the ground.

Rikard was across the room in a flash. He picked her up and threw her headfirst into the closet, smashing the glass to bits. A few of the other vampires were home and though they heard the commotion, none would interfere. Rikard didn't take kindly to anyone getting involved in his affairs.

Franciska's face was bloody and filled with shards of glass. It didn't matter. She would be all healed up in a few hours after he was through venting. It didn't make sense for her to fight back. Rikard was a powerful one hundred and forty year old vampire. He could easily kill her. But she knew that he wouldn't. After his jealous rage he would calm down and cry, asking her why she couldn't love him.

Her mind was on Laku, even as Rikard picked her up, ripped her clothes off, shoved her onto the bed and entered her from behind. Laku's transformation would be soon complete. It had been eight hours now since she left Paris by train. At the rate the venom had assimilated itself in his blood stream, it could very well be over in another couple of hours. It was incredible. It was as though Laku was meant to be a vampire.

Rikard, his fury increasing at her lack of response to him, twisted her head all the way around so that she was now looking at him though he was still behind her.

"*Kurva utallak!*" he hissed angrily, choking her as he drilled her insides mercilessly.

The choking was merely symbolic of his anger. It had no effect on Franciska. Vampires only breathed out of habit, not necessity.

All Franciska could think about was Laku.

She wondered for the thousandth time since she left him writhing on his bed in agony, if she had made the right decision.

Surely staying, and being inevitably destroyed with him, would be better than living forever without him.

She screamed in frustration.

Chapter 13

The pain stopped abruptly. Laku got up from off the floor where he had ended up after rolling off the bed at some point during the transformation. The first thing that he became aware of was his acutely sharpened senses. He could hear the wind whispering against the trees outside. He could smell the earth, and knew that it had rained. His body felt light, yet he felt so strong. He was also thirsty. Blood thirsty. During one of their long talks, Franciska had told him what it was like for the first seven months to a year, when a human became a vampire. The lack of control. The unquenchable thirst for human blood. The violence.

The first year was brutal for a newborn. And she had left him to deal with it by himself. She knew how much he loved her. And she told him that she loved him. Yet it wasn't enough to persuade her to stay. She was gone. She had bit him and exited his life as quickly as she had entered it.

If only the memory of her could disappear just as quickly, Laku thought bitterly. But it wouldn't. He would never be able to forget her. She had changed his life and there was no going back.

He walked over to the mirror. He could see his reflection. At least for the time being. Franciska had told him that excess human blood remained in a newborn for months. Until he was completely devoid of it, he would still have some human characteristics.

Despite his turmoil and heartache, he was fascinated by the image staring back at him. He knew that as a human he had been a very handsome man. He was now an extraordinarily handsome vampire. His face was simply mesmerizing. His blood red eyes were an intense contrast to his now waxen-like caramel skin.

The thirst was steadily building up. He knew that he would have to soon obey its call. He was now at the top of the food chain. He would have to kill people to satisfy his hunger. He was now a predator. The reality hit him like a ton of bricks. He turned away from the mirror, suddenly feeling confused. Ashamed. Lost. Angry.

Intensely disturbed, Laku got dressed. He pulled on a pair of gray Dior jeans, black Aldo boots, a black sweater with a hood and a black Vuitton trench coat with gold buttons.

At least I haven't lost my sense of style Laku mused wryly, as he pulled the hood over his head and exited the house, stepping out into the cold December air.

He strode dazedly out into his new world.

Laku was assaulted by the overwhelming scent of human blood as he drove down the quiet street of his picturesque neighbourhood. It took all of his willpower to pass by houses that he knew were occupied by people filled with the warm inviting blood that he craved so much. It was pure torture. It was a lesson in control. It would not do for him to feed anywhere near the wealthy area in which he resided. With a gargantuan effort, he managed to make it out of Isle Saint-Louis.

Laku headed to Chez Prune, a renovated bar on rue Beaurepaire in the Canal St. Martin area. He parked on the side of the street and slipped on a pair of Dolce & Gabbana glasses that had a light reddish tint. They would help to not make his eyes seem so red. He exited the car and slipped off the hood of his sweater.

He strolled into the bar and blended in with the artsy designer crowd. He immediately became aware of one his new powers. He could read people's thoughts. Then he realized that wasn't entirely true. He could only read someone's mind if the person was thinking about him. Like the pretty brunette in the red cardigan and skinny jeans standing with two other women. She had been in a conversation with them but she was no longer listening.

She had noticed Laku and was instantly drawn to what she was sure was the most handsome man that she had ever laid eyes upon. She mentally raped him and had the residue in her white panties to prove it.

Qúest-ce qúun morceau á chaud! Je lui baise dans un battement de coeur!

Aren't we horny, Laku thought in amusement as he walked by slowly, treating her to smile that made her drink almost slip from her hand. She watched as he walked around the corner where the restrooms were located.

"Je serai bientot de retour..." she said to her friends, placing her drink on the bar counter. *"Je vais aux toilettes."*

The young woman, Josiane, was a ballet dancer with the Ballet National de Marseille, a world-class dance company. She was having a rare night out with friends, enjoying the first of her three days off.

Her heart pounding with excitement at the possibilities of this unexpected adventure, she made her way around the corner. She had never done anything like this before. But there was something so seductive about the handsome stranger that she just couldn't resist. Besides, you only lived once. She wanted him to stuff her panties in her mouth to muffle her cries of passion as he pounded her in the confines of one of the stalls. The throbbing between her legs intensified at the thought.

She went into the men's room. Laku was standing by the last stall. There was no one else inside the restroom. He watched as she approached him, her veins pumping with nervous excitement. Her face was flushed and her eyes were glazed with passion.

Having held off for so long, Laku was now struggling mightily to control himself. The thirst had reached its zenith. But he didn't want to spoil the moment by just jumping on her and ravaging her right in the middle of the restroom. Besides, someone could very well just walk in and that would create a huge problem. He knew exactly how he wanted the next two minutes to unfold.

He stared at her intensely and she swooned when she got closer, falling against him. She was weak with passion and raging desire. Laku held her and opened the door to the stall. He pulled her in and locked the door behind them.

He kissed her forcefully, hungrily, devouring her mouth with primal vigor. Josiane groaned in his mouth. She swore she was going to have an orgasm just from his passionate kisses.

Laku ended the kiss and spun her around. She braced against the wall with her hands, as Laku pulled her jeans and underwear down in one fluid movement. His mouth at her neck, fangs bared and ready, he unzipped his jeans and pulled out his erection. He rubbed it against her dripping wetness as he licked her neck, relishing her scent, her taste. He entered her with a firm, hard thrust.

"Oui! Oui! Oh mon dieu!"

Josiane gasped in amazement. She was coming. He had only been inside her for mere seconds. She was about to scream as her orgasm shook her to the core when Laku covered her mouth with one hand and sank his teeth into her neck viciously. Josiane immediately tumbled from her cloud of ecstasy. In a split second she went from experiencing the quickest, most intense orgasm that she had ever had, to enduring the most excruciating pain that she had ever felt.

Laku gorged on her thrashing body, drinking hungrily, thirstily, until there was no more.

With blood trickling down his chin, he looked down on the mutilated corpse partially propped up by the toilet.

He had done it. His first kill. He felt a mixture of euphoria and disgust. Euphoria at having his first exquisite taste of human blood, disgust that he had taken a life to get it. He had been a human less than twenty four hours ago. Thinking of them as food would take some getting used to. This had been a young woman with a life, a family, goals and dreams. And now she was gone.

He would have willingly become a vampire to be able to be with Franciska forever. But with her out of the picture, everything had changed. He didn't want this. Why had she done this to him if she knew that she wasn't going to stay? So what if she had feared Rikard would find out about him and kill him? At this point he would welcome death rather than being this monster. This abomination that Franciska had turned him into and left behind.

He hated her.

He loved her.

He hated that he loved her.

He hated himself for loving her.

Chapter 14

Laku slipped his dick inside his jeans and pulled the zipper up. He exited the bathroom and went over to the face basin. He turned on the tap and washed the blood from off his mouth and hands.

One of the stalls opened and a short, compact man in ridiculously tight jeans came out humming a tune.

He sized Laku up openly as he washed his hands.

"Bonjour il ya," he said, in a high pitched voice.

Laku ignored him, as he studied his reflection in the mirror. He was still wearing his tinted shades. His mouth was now devoid of blood but the same couldn't be said for his sweater and coat. But he was in all black and it wasn't very noticeable. He needed to leave though. The body would probably be soon discovered. He walked out of the bathroom, ignoring the man's thoughts. If he paid any attention to them, he would lose it and rip his head off.

Laku walked by the two girls that the girl he had just killed was hanging with when he entered the bar. They were still in animated conversation. Laku made his way through the crowd and exited the bar.

As he walked to his car he was disturbingly sure of one thing.

As guilty and disgusted as he felt about killing the young woman, she would not be his only victim tonight.

He was still thirsty.

A lanky real estate lawyer went into the restroom. The first three stalls were occupied and one guy was at the urinal yapping on his cell phone as he urinated. He knocked on the door of the last stall and realized that it wasn't locked. He opened it and froze in fright.

"Pere miséricordieux..." he whispered hoarsely, crossing his chest as he backed out of the stall, horrified by the grotesque sight in front of him.

His bladder was unable to withstand the pressure. The front of his dark denim became a shade darker as his bladder emptied itself of the cognac that he had been drinking. He stood in front of the stall and pointed in front of him with a trembling hand. A man entered the bathroom, just as another was exiting one of the stalls. They both looked at the lawyer in alarm, wondering what the hell was wrong with him.

"Êtes-vous autorisé monsieur?" one of them asked, as they both approached him warily.

They looked where he was pointing and one of them threw up the half-bottle of red wine that he had consumed, splashing the shoes and pants of the guy that had originally discovered the body.

The guy at the urinal finished peeing and turned around. The phone fell from his hand in mid-conversation, smashing to bits on the ceramic tile, as he stared at the bloody, half-naked body in the stall.

Someone rushed out to call security.

Laku got home at three a.m. He went straight to the laundry room and dumped his clothes inside the washing machine. He usually took most of his clothing to the cleaners but that would not be possible, at least not with the clothes he wore when out feeding. All that blood would definitely raise some eyebrows at the cleaners. Better to be careful and launder them at home.

He went into the bathroom and turned on the shower. His thirst was temporarily quenched, but it had taken four people to do it. After leaving the bar, he claimed a victim over by Pigalle Place, a cute young prostitute who had solicited him, and finally, a lesbian couple on their way to their car after leaving Madam, a gay club on rue La Boetie.

The latter had been a messy affair, as one of them had managed to run off before he caught her and finished her off. There was blood all over the parking lot and having stuffed the two bodies underneath two cars, they had most likely already been discovered.

Laku sighed as the water cascaded down his ripped frame. He had killed four humans tonight. He was a murderer. He had been a very civilized well-bred human. The transition into a bloodthirsty, murderous monster was not a smooth one.

He turned off the water and stepped out of the shower. He dried himself with a large red towel, and wrapping it around his waist, he went over to the full-length mirror. His eyes, now crimson, stared back at him as if desperately asking for answers. He had none. He had come to grips with an identity crisis, and he could not allow the crisis to win. He would have to get used to his new eating habits. He could only hope that it would be sooner than later. The first step would be to better control his thirst. That would lead to feeding less, and also allow him to feed in a more controlled setting, where the bodies wouldn't be discovered.

He had always been strong and he needed his inner strength now more than ever. He had been left on his own to deal with this curse, or gift, depending on how he chose to look at it. Life was all about perspective, wasn't it? These were the cards that he had been dealt and he had to play out his hand. He would have to

adapt. Adjust. Accept. Embrace it even. It wouldn't
be easy. Would probably be as difficult as France's national soccer team winning back their fans after their
shameful debacle at the World Cup in South Africa, but
he could do it. Had to do it. And it all began with his
perception of himself.

He maintained eye contact with his image.

I am not a monster.

I'm an alternate form of human.

Chapter 15

Franciska sighed as she read the newspaper article. She was in Lajos' room, reading news stories online on his laptop. Lajos was the youngest vampire in the coven and used to be a graphic designer before he became a vampire. He was the only one in the coven who had a computer. He still did graphics work, mostly album covers for rock bands and posters for promoters of rock concerts. He had clients from all over, none of whom had ever met him face to face. He conducted all of his business through his website.

There had been four brutal murders in different sections of Paris last night and based on the wounds, the police were speculating that the murders were carried out by the same person or persons, according to the article which was written by a French reporter. A policeman was quoted as saying that only a wild animal, most likely a wolf, could have killed these people so viciously. He was unable to say how a wolf, or any wild animal for that matter, had gotten into a trendy Paris bar and killed a woman in the bathroom while having sex with her.

Franciska shook her head.

Idiota.

Laku. He was out quenching his thirst last night. She hoped that he would be able to learn to feed without attracting attention. If he continued to rack up the death count like this, it would only be a matter of time before the Chosen Ones stepped in.

She missed him so much. She would give anything to be with him right now.

Anything.

She wondered how he felt about her now. He was no doubt heartbroken that she had left him but surely he still loved her. True love never truly dies. She wondered what his special talents were like. There was no doubt in her mind that he definitely had an abundance of special powers that the average vampire could only dream of. Laku had been an extraordinary human. He must be a very special vampire. Look how quickly his transformation had taken place. Franciska was still amazed at that.

"Franciska! Gyere ide!" she heard from the hallway. Rikard was calling her. She sighed, closed the article and got up. Rikard wanted to kill Laku but surprisingly, he

could only see Laku's face through her eyes, he couldn't track him or tap into his energy. Apparently one of Laku's new gifts was that he was impervious to mental probing. She wondered if that gift was powerful enough to prevent even the Chosen Ones from invading his mind. If so, that was incredible. And even more evidence that she had made the wrong choice in leaving him.

"Franciska!"

She got up and left the room to see what Rikard wanted. Probably nothing. He was driving her crazy ever since she got back from Paris. Last night he had demanded that she take him to Paris to find Laku. She told him that she didn't know where to find him. Rikard knew that she was lying but like she told him when he pressed and got physical, hurting her would not make her do it. He could kill her for all she cared. She was so depressed and missed Laku so much that she would welcome death. It would be better than this dull existence and the constant painful ache in her heart. She was stupid and naïve to think that she could go back to her life after sharing what she shared with Laku.

There was no going back.

Rikard was standing by their bedroom door waiting for her.

He pulled her inside and locked the door.

Laku was painting when he heard a rare sound. The telephone was ringing. Very few people had his home number and he rarely used cell phones. He didn't like the idea of people being able to reach him at all times. He was tempted to ignore it but got up and in a split second, he was by the antique phone, a 1930s model. He already knew who it was. He picked up the receiver and answered it.

"*Bonjour.*"

"*Salut, Laku.*"

It was Gabrielle. He had not seen or spoken to her in over two months. She wanted to come over. It was weird having a telephone conversation when you already knew what the other person was thinking and what they were going to say before they said it.

"*Venez me voir.*" He invited her over not because he really wanted to see her but because it would be a good test in his quest to control his urges. Making love to Gabrielle without turning her into dinner would be a good sign.

"*ll ok je vous vois en vingt minutes.*"

Laku hung up without saying anything further. He could feel her excitement; hear the things she planned to do to him. The things she wanted him to do to her.

Ah, Gabrielle.

It was going to be a very interesting evening.

Chapter 16

"Mmmm..." Gabrielle moaned as Laku fondled her breasts. *"Ca fait tellement longtemps..."*

She had arrived at his home a few minutes ago and had entered the house to find him lying in bed naked, waiting for her, his erection raging. Pleasantly surprised that he seemed to miss her as much as she missed him, she had quickly undressed and joined him in the bed.

She marveled at how *hard* his shaft was as she caressed it. It felt like marble. She couldn't recall ever feeling a dick so hard. Matter of fact, his entire body was ridiculously hard. Other things were different too. His voice, which was always sexy to begin with, now had an even more melodic and seductive tone to it. When he spoke to her it sent shivers down her spine. His touch was ice cold. Yet it warmed her inside. Kissing him was like sucking on a popsicle that was filled with warm honey. Everything just seemed and felt so incredibly intense. Her senses were overwhelmed.

She was dripping wet.

She needed him inside her.

Now.

She climbed on top of him and impaled herself on his rigid member, gasping as it filled her up.

"Oui...oui...oh Laku...ca fait du bien..." Gabrielle moaned as she moved her waist in a circular motion, grinding her way to ecstasy. Her head was thrown back and she rubbed her small breasts as she felt her climax steadily approaching. *"Oh mon dieu...tu vas me faire venire si dur!"*

Laku looked up at her trembling form as she climaxed. She was totally caught up in rapture. Her eyes were closed and her teeth tightly clenched. Her breathing was laboured and her face was flushed pink.

He gazed at her elegant neck wistfully but the urge was not unbearable. He was in total control. Still deeply embedded inside her, Laku rose and stepped off the bed. Gabrielle gasped. She was not the heaviest woman in the world but Laku moved from off the bed effortlessly like there wasn't a grown woman on his dick.

Her head spun as he moved around the room with her, bringing her up and down, over and over again, making her grunt and moan with pleasure. It felt like they were floating around the room. Gabrielle was sure that she was delirious. A heavy wave of euphoria washed over her as she climaxed for the third time that evening.

It was like having an orgasm in 3D.

It was more intense than anything that she had ever experienced.

She lost consciousness.

Laku heard an unfamiliar sound for the second time that day. His doorbell was ringing. That was indeed a rarity. Even more so than the ringing of his telephone. He was lying in bed nude, thinking. Gabrielle had gone home an hour ago, completely sated, utterly amazed and a tad bit confused. It had been a satisfying but peculiar two hours she had spent with Laku and he had sent her home, ignoring the questions in her eyes. He was pleased with himself. He was now positive that he would be able to control his thirst, and quench it only when it was convenient. Franciska had told him that newborns were uncontrollable in the first year. He was already realizing he was not a typical vampire. It made perfect sense to him. He had never been a typical man to begin with.

The doorbell chimed again. Laku got up and put on a robe. In a second he was at the door. He opened it just as the person was about to ring it again.

"Bonsoir, Paul-Henri," Laku said, greeting his late evening visitor with a hearty handshake. He had not seen him since the funeral service for his parents over two years ago. Paul-Henri Moreau was a Brigadier of the Police Nationale, a longtime friend of the Leon family – he had been close to Laku's father, and the person who had called Laku to advise him of his parent's demise.

He was taken aback by the unusual colour of Laku's eyes. They were crimson.

"Lentille de contact," Laku explained.

Paul-Henri winced slightly at the coldness of Laku's hand and the strength of his handshake.

"Laku...ll a été depuis longtemps. Bon de vous voir." He smiled but Laku knew that he was troubled. This was not a social call.

Laku invited him in and closed the door. They went into the living room and Laku told him to have a seat. The fireplace was not lit but the heat was on. Laku had turned it on for Gabrielle's benefit and had not turned it off when she left.

"Voulez-vous quelque chose a boire?" Laku asked, walking over to the mini-bar.

"Oui, je vous remercie," Paul-Henri responded, as he sat down on the couch. His doctor had told him to lay off the alcohol on his last visit a month ago but he had had only one drink since then. Surely another wouldn't hurt. If his fifty-three year old liver was already

bad, the occasional drink would hardly make it any worse.

Laku poured them brandy and handed him a glass.

Laku sat across from Paul-Henri and sipped his drink, studying him as he waited patiently for him to get to the reason for his visit. He was not aging well. In two years he had aged rapidly. He looked much older than his fifty-three years. His face was deeply wrinkled, his teeth sported coffee and tobacco stains, and his hairline was now miles away from his prominent forehead. Not so long ago he had been a good looking man. That man was now gone.

Paul-Henri's thoughts were swirling as he struggled for the right way to tell Laku what he had to say. The reports of the grisly murders the other night had landed on his desk and in two of the murders, the one in the bathroom at the bar, and the one of the prostitute in Pigalle Place, eyewitnesses had spoken of seeing a tall, handsome man in the vicinity close to the time of the murders.

The description had uncannily fit Laku. He had initially dismissed it as a coincidence but it had been gnawing at him and he finally decided to pay Laku a surprise visit. But now that he was here, he wasn't sure how to broach the topic. Laku was almost like a godson to him, though since his dear parents died he had cut himself off from everyone, and he wasn't the most sociable person to begin with. Laku had always been a loner.

He was a hit with the ladies but he wasn't the type of person who had many friends.

Paul-Henri took a hearty sip of his drink. There was no way that Laku could have been mixed up in those brutal murders, but as a policeman, he had to clear his conscience and at least speak to him. He was uncomfortable with the smug way in which Laku was looking at him, like they shared a secret. It was as if Laku knew what he was thinking.

He suddenly felt very cold and afraid.

He wanted nothing more than to leave.

He downed his drink and was about to uneasily broach the topic when he felt a sharp pain in his head. It was so brief that he wondered if he had imagined it.

For a second there he was sure that he had something to talk to Laku about, but for the life of him, he couldn't remember what it was. He was also suddenly very relaxed.

He shrugged and asked Laku how he had been doing.

Chapter 17

Three nights after Paul-Henri's visit, Laku decided to go on the street. He left the house at 2 a.m. He did not drive. He felt like walking, embracing the night. It was bitterly cold, and windy, further evidence that Christmas was only a couple of weeks away. Laku was oblivious to both facts. The weather didn't affect him, and he had not cared about Christmas since his parents died. Their accident had occurred on Christmas Eve two and a half years ago, forever changing the way he felt about that time of the year.

As he walked by the famed Notre Dame Cathedral, he absently wondered what would happen to him if he tried to enter a church. He didn't intend to find out. His parents were Catholic but had not been overly religious. He had not considered himself to be of any particular faith, and had read widely about the various religions, in an attempt to arrive at his own truth, glean his own understanding. He had studied the Bible, the Qur'an, the Vedas, the complete Buddhist Sutra collection and many other religious texts. It was a fascinating, ongoing journey. One he wondered if it made sense continuing in his present state. Perhaps not. It would only lead to guilt and confusion, and he was already on the road of being at peace with himself, with what he now was.

He reflected on Paul-Henri's visit as he continued his aimless early morning stroll. He was moving quickly, effortlessly, and had covered a lot of ground in mere minutes. He was now in the northwest of the Ninth Arrondissement, in Place de Clichy, popular for its famous Moulin Rouge and bustling nightlife.

Laku was discovering more and more of his newly acquired talents. During Paul-Henri's visit, he had found out that he could rid someone's consciousness of a particular thought or memory. He had read Paul-Henri's mind and on a whim, attempted to banish his thoughts. It had worked like a charm, requiring just a few seconds of intense concentration. Apparently it was painful for the person, Paul-Henri's eyes had bulged unnaturally and he had grunted in pain, but it was brief.

Suddenly sensing a presence that posed danger, Laku stopped abruptly. He was standing at one of the many crossroads that characterized the area. There were several people milling about, but he picked out the threat immediately. He had always wondered if there were other vampires in Paris. His question was answered. There were four of them, three males and one female, standing about thirty meters away. They were watching him intently. Interestingly, he could tell that the female was the leader of the pack.

He could read their minds. They had suspected that he was a vampire by how quickly and effortlessly he had been walking. Their suspicion had been confirmed when he had sensed their presence and looked over at them, and they saw his eyes.

The leader was perplexed. She could tell that Laku was a newborn because of the colour of his eyes but even as he stood there, still as a statue, she could not sense his presence. That was very unusual. There was something different about this one. He exhibited no outward sign of fear. Where had he come from and what was he doing in their territory?

They would capture him, interrogate him, and make him a part of the coven. He was the most handsome creature she had ever seen in her one hundred and twenty-five years. She would take him as her mate. Thierry would be upset but she was the leader, whatever she said was law.

Laku moved quickly.

"Allons!" the woman, Marie-Elise, hissed as they ran after him, marveling at his superior speed.

None of them had ever seen a vampire move that fast. They would not be able to catch him.

They were now in the Les Halles area, a known enclave of criminal activity. They moved through the pockets of drug dealers and their customers, and the strange looking individuals that frequented the area, and just when they thought that they had lost him, to their surprise, he was standing in an alley, apparently waiting for them.

Marie-Elise knew that this would not go as smoothly as she had initially thought but she was confident that they would prevail. Thierry was also a newborn and was very strong. The four of them should be able to take him.

They entered the alley cautiously but confidently.

Chapter 18

"*Qui etes-vous?*" Marie-Elise asked, as she stood twenty feet from Laku, flanked by the other three vampires.

Laku did not respond. He merely stood there, looking at them with a stoic expression. He already knew where this was heading. And he was ready to go there.

"*Oú êtes-vous?*" she continued, when he did not respond.

Ten tension-filled seconds ticked by slowly before Thierry hissed and bared his fangs. He was ready for action. He could sense that Marie-Elise was impressed by this strange vampire. He was having none of it. He would show her that he could subdue him and teach him how to talk seeing as he seems to have forgotten how to do so.

"*Je vais le faire parler,*" Thierry said, looking at Marie-Elise for permission. She gave him the slightest of nods, without taking her eyes from off of Laku. He was so handsome and hot it was unreal. His nonchalant attitude in the face of danger turned her on immensely. She had never met anyone like him, man or vampire. She desired him.

Thierry crouched, his red eyes blazing with hatred for this handsome rogue that had peaked the interest of his woman. He couldn't wait to teach him a lesson.

Laku continued to stand upright, his only discernable movement was to bare his fangs.

Thierry sprang. Laku moved so fast that he was a blur. He met Thierry in mid-air and flung him into the side wall of the building on the left. Thierry released a gut wrenching scream as he slammed into the wall, breaking several of the bricks.

He was missing his right arm.

It was wiggling in Laku's hand.

Laku broke it into several more pieces and threw them behind him.

Marie-Elise was stunned.

He had just discarded a very strong newborn so effortlessly it was like he had merely swatted a fly. She looked over at Thierry. He was still screaming and his eyes were blazing with fury, but he did not attack again. He knew that he would be killed.

The other two vampires did not wait for Marie-Elise to give them permission. Hissing savagely, they attacked Laku in unison. Laku met them in mid-flight and when he descended to the ground, he held both of their heads in his hands like two bloody trophies. The two headless bodies wandered around in a frenzy, hitting over garbage cans, each other and banging into the wall.

Looking at the woman, he smashed them together until the pieces scattered like a jigsaw puzzle. The headless bodies crumbled to the ground.

The screaming of the wounded vampire was getting to him. He sprang onto him and finished the job, using his incredible strength to rip him in two from the torso. Then he dropped the top half and leaping high into the air, came down viciously on Thierry's face, crushing it to bits.

Marie-Elise was in a state of shock. The strange vampire had obliterated her coven in the flash of an eye. She looked at the carnage. They were dead. They had been broken into too many pieces for them to ever recover. The sun would take care of their remains in the morning.

She was now alone.

She stared at the expressionless stranger.

In ten short minutes he had turned her world upside down and had yet to even utter a word.

She knew that she couldn't outrun him and she was not strong enough to fight him.

The ball was in his court.

Chapter 19

"*Oh mon dieu! Oui! Oui! Donnez-le moi!*" Marie-Elise screamed passionately as Laku stroked her fast and furious. She had been on top of him, riding her way to her second quick orgasm, and when she got there, she suddenly found her back against the ceiling as she climaxed violently, with Laku still inside her, filling her like she had never been filled, pumping away, his arms and feet on the ceiling, holding them up high above the bed.

It was the most incredible thing she had ever witnessed.

It was the most incredible orgasm she had ever experienced.

From certain death to excruciating pleasure.

She had been certain that he was going to kill her. Instead, after staring her down for thirty long seconds, while her existence hung in the balance, he had taken her home and introduced her to the type of sex she never knew existed. He had yet to utter a word to her. In the alley he had merely taken her by the arm and in fifteen minutes they were in his spacious bedroom, having futuristic sex.

She climaxed in mid-air as Laku took them back down to the bed, turning them around so that she was now on her back. He threw her long legs on his shoulders and continued to pound her into orgasmic submission.

"Je viens á nouveau...Je viens á nouveau...oui... oui..." Marie-Elise croaked as yet another orgasm wracked her soulless body. She was completely under Laku's spell. His dick was like a magic wand, granting her orgasm after orgasm.

Marie-Elise had heard of multiple orgasms but this was ridiculous. She had climaxed more in the past half hour than she had in over a hundred years of getting laid. She didn't even care that Laku had killed her lover and the rest of her coven. All that mattered at this moment was that she was with him. The most handsome, virile, strange being she had ever encountered.

She didn't want this night to end.

But it would.

Laku flipped her over and pulled her to her knees. He pummeled her from behind and as he gave her one hard, final thrust, he held her head with both hands and separated it from her body.

He held it in the air and looked into her eyes, frozen forever in orgasmic bliss.

She never saw it coming.

He pulled out of her headless body and took her remains out to the fireplace.

Laku, having showered and wearing a white Hermes bathrobe, opened a bottle of Petrus vintage and poured a glass. He sat in his favourite chair and sipped the wine as Marie-Elise's remains burned in the fireplace. Having a drink was a habit that he didn't intend to break. The impressive wine collection would not go to waste. He would indulge every now and then, even if he no longer had the taste for anything other than blood.

The woman was gone. Only her ashes remained as proof that she had ever existed. He didn't even know her name. The only reason that he hadn't killed her in the alley along with the rest of her coven was that he wanted to know what it was like to have sex with another vampire. To be able to be himself without having to hold back. To be as primal and as savage as he wanted, and release the undead beast that he truly was; and experiment with all sorts of spectacular moves that would have freaked out a human. He had thoroughly enjoyed the experience. It had proven to be quite liberating. But there was never any doubt that he would have killed her after he was through.

Under the circumstances which they met, there was no way he could allow her to live.

At least she had died a beautiful death.

He finished his drink and padded to his studio.

He felt like painting.

Chapter 20

Three months had passed since the fateful day that Franciska bit Laku and left Paris, changing both their lives forever. Not a single day passed that she was not tormented by her decision to go back to Hungary. It was the biggest mistake that she had ever made in her life. Before meeting Laku, she had been relatively contented. Her life wasn't particularly exciting, or fulfilling, but it had been sufficient.

Her experience with Laku had showed her that she wasn't living. She had been merely existing; going with the flow like a dead fish.

She had gotten a taste of real love. She knew what it was like for someone to love her so unconditionally that he would change and risk his life just so that he could be with her. She had briefly experienced what it was like to face each day filled with unadulterated joy, to be blissfully happy. She had discovered what it was like to give and receive unbridled passion, to have sex that was so magical it seemed unreal.

Yet she had walked away from it all, thinking that it was the best decision.

She was so stupid.

And she was paying dearly for her stupidity. She simply could not go on like this. She was lost. Dreadfully sad. Listless. Angry. Disgusted with herself. And she hated Rikard. He didn't love her. She had come to realize that now. He was obsessed with her. If he loved her he would let her go. He knew how miserable and unhappy she was. And he knew why. Yet he didn't care as long as he had her. She was his prisoner. Until the end of time.

She had contemplated running away to Laku many times. But two things stopped her. It was practically impossible to get away from Rikard. He was watching her like a hawk. And even if she did manage to elude him and get to Paris, which was highly unlikely, she wasn't sure if Laku would welcome her with open arms. After all, she had betrayed his love and his trust.

The look on his face and the utter dismay in his eyes when he realized that she was leaving him haunted her every single moment of every passing day. It had become unbearable.

She simply could not take it anymore.

She knew what she had to do.

She made her way to the bedroom.

"Utállak!" Franciska snarled, as she stood at the door and glared at Rikard. He was sitting up in bed, smoking a cigarette. He looked at her in amusement. So what if she hated him. She would hate him even more if he could get his hands on the man in Paris that had taken her away from him. He would rip him to shreds. She was here only in the physical. Her heart and her mind were still in Paris. But it mattered not. She would never have him. They would never be together. She was going to stay right here by his side, whether she wanted to or not.

In an instant Franciska was on top of him, her red eyes blazing like two spectacular balls of fire. She snatched the cigarette from his hand and pressed the burning end into his left eye. Rikard squealed and slapped her viciously. She was hurled through the open door, and hit the wall in the passageway hard, cracking it in several places. But she would not be deterred. She sprang to her feet and attacked him again, her anger and frustration making her even stronger than usual. She knew that she was no match for him, but she was going to kill him or die trying.

It was the only way out.

His death or hers.

"*Te örült ribanc!*" Rikard shouted, as he met her in mid-air and kicked her in the throat. Franciska smashed into the glass of the recently repaired closet door.

She was back on her feet immediately, crouched and ready to launch another attack.

"*Én figyelmeztetem Franciska! Allj, mielött igazán bántani!*" Rikard warned, his wounded eye already beginning to heal.

He was alarmed and amazed at her reckless behaviour. He had never seen her act like this before.

Franciska ignored his warning and reached into the waist of her trousers and removed a slender, sharpened wooden stake. She was going to put it through his evil heart.

"*Baszd meg!*" she growled as she launched her final, determined attack.

Rikard's thin lips were curled in an angry sneer. He couldn't believe that she really wanted to kill him. Ungrateful bitch. He had found her near dead, healed her, given her the gift of eternal life and this was how she repaid him. By falling in love with another man and attempting to kill him so that she would be free to be with that man.

A rage unlike any that he had ever experienced overcame him and he emitted a blood-curling growl that reeked of frustration, hurt and anger.

Faster than Franciska, he sidestepped her vicious lunge and threw her headfirst into the wall. Her neck snapped like a twig. As she attempted to rise again, her head leaning at an awkward angle, Rikard was on top of her, furious beyond reason. He punched her repeatedly, until her face was a bloody pulp. He then gouged out her eyes and tore her nose from off her face.

Finally, with bloody tears streaming down his hollowed cheeks, he took the stake from her hand, which was still stubbornly gripping it with all her remaining strength, and stabbed her in the heart.

A grotesque semblance of a smile came over what was left of Franciska's face just before she disintegrated into nothing.

She was free at last.

Rikard wept uncontrollably.

Then he took the stake and thrust it into his heart.

Chapter 21

It was exactly one year to the day that Laku met Franciska on that windswept Friday night outside of Showcase. He was back at the club, feeling nostalgic as he sat alone in a private booth upstairs, an untouched bottle of Armand de Brignac champagne in a bucket on the table in front of him. This section was reserved for celebrities. He was a celebrity, though not the type that the bouncer or the cute hostess would recognize. A little mental persuasion had done the trick.

The bouncer had pulled the red velvet rope back and allowed him in with a nod, and the hostess had greeted him with a warm smile and escorted him to the small, secluded booth, one of several in that section. The booth was fully decorated in white and consisted of a circular white leather couch with a glass table designed like a star in front of it. It could comfortably accommodate five people.

Laku didn't know why, but the urge to go back there had been so strong that he couldn't ignore it. He missed Franciska, and he still loved her – that would never change – but she didn't dominate his thoughts. It had taken several months, but he was no longer angry at her betrayal. He had forgiven her for leaving him. What was love without forgiveness?

He had contemplated on several occasions going to Budapest to look for her. He would find her and bring her back, and kill Rikard and the entire coven if they tried to stop him, which they undoubtedly would. He was certain that she had realized the error of her ways, and would have gladly returned if she could. There was only one problem. No matter how hard he tried, he couldn't tap into her energy. Without that it would be impossible for him to find her. It was as though she was no longer in existence. He had shuddered at the thought and dismissed it. But why couldn't he reach her?

The hostess pulled the thin, white curtains and stuck her long neck in.

"*Puis-je vous quelque chose?*"

"*Non, je vais bien.*"

She looked at him searchingly before nodding and walking away.

Laku could her hear thoughts loud and clear. Perhaps he would indeed give her what she desired. And then take what he desired.

He had not fed in close to a month.
It was about time.

Laku opened the bottle of champagne, and poured himself a drink. He took a sip and reflected on the past year. Meeting Franciska had been the defining moment in his life. He was now a fully fledged vampire, all trace of human blood had been gone from his body from as early as four months after he was bitten. Since his initial feeding frenzy, he had successfully learnt how to control his urges, instead of being controlled by them. He now only fed once or twice per month, and there was never any risk of discovery, as he took his victims home and disposed of them in his fireplace when he was through. They were simply reported as missing.

He was cognizant that as powerful as he was, he might have more at his disposal of which he was not yet aware. They would manifest in due time, if and when they were needed.

And last but not least, he had embraced his fate.

He was at peace with himself.

And it showed in his artistry. He had painted more in the past year than he had done in his entire life. He had eighty-five new paintings, including twenty terrifyingly brilliant pieces that he named *Les Morts Vivants,* The Living Dead. He was tempted to contact his long time agent and have an exhibition. He knew that he had produced some of his finest, darkest work, and he wanted to share some of it with the art world. He doubted that he would attend but it wouldn't matter. Everyone who was anyone in the art world would be there to view his masterpieces. An exhibition from Laku Leon was about as common as common sense. They wouldn't miss it for the world.

He felt like taking a trip. He wanted to go somewhere far away and exotic. Have an adventure. Do something different. He would go to an island. Tahiti. Bali. Fiji. Hawaii. The Bahamas. Santorini.

Then it hit him.

Jamaica.

He would go to Jamaica.

A vampire on vacation in the Caribbean.

It should be a very interesting trip.

Chapter 22

Chasity sighed as she watched the cursor on her Sony Vaio laptop blink at her mockingly. She was trying to get going on her third book but she was feeling uninspired. It had been like this for the past two months. She was getting worried. She wasn't used to having writer's block and it was making her anxious and depressed.

Her first novel, *The Flying Ostrich*, a quirky contemporary romance tale, was an instant success. The publisher who took a chance on the then twenty-three old freelance graphic designer who had convinced him with her raw talent and quiet confidence, had only done an initial print run of 1500 copies. After favourable reviews in the local newspapers, word of mouth, and creating a buzz online through Facebook, sales were brisk and another 5000 copies were quickly printed.

Chasity avoided the dreaded sophomore slump a year and a half later with her second novel, *Life Interrupted,* a dark romance drama which was nominated for The Miller-Ramdon Prize which was awarded to the best novel of the year written by a citizen of the British Commonwealth. She did not win but being nominated and making the short list for the prestigious prize afforded her a lot of free international publicity that resulted in strong sales in markets where she was previously unheard of.

Her publisher was on her case. It was time to begin her third book, which was tentatively titled *Shackles,* a tale of a woman trapped in an unhappy marriage with a sadistic pastor. But the book was not cooperating. Her creative well was as dry as an eighty year old woman's vagina. Chasity sighed and got up from around the desk.

She went out to the kitchen and retrieved her chilled bottle of white wine. Her home phone rang as she poured a glass. It rang out and started ringing again by the time she got to it.

It was Jameer, her boyfriend.

"Hey you," Chasity said, taking a sip of her wine as she made her way back to the spare bedroom that doubled as her office. She lived in a two bedroom apartment in Kensington Clove, a gated apartment complex off Old Hope Road. The rent was expensive but it was worth it. The complex was centrally located, safe and comprised of mostly upwardly mobile professionals.

"Just checking if you're home. I'm coming over."

Chasity tried not to get annoyed. Yes it was a Friday night but she had already told Jameer that she was going to try and get some writing done, and that she would see him tomorrow. Apparently he had amnesia.

"Babe, I told you I'd be writing tonight," she reminded him gently, trying not to start an argument. Jameer had a quick temper and she really didn't want to fight with him tonight. They had been doing way too much of that lately.

"Look I miss you and I want to see you. I'm already on my way. We haven't hooked up all week. Sometimes I really have to wonder if you're cheating on me."

Chasity sighed in exasperation. *Here we go again.* She really didn't need this right now. The bigger her career got, the more jealous and insecure Jameer became. She was a very attractive girl who wrote sexy, edgy books. She got a lot of attention from male admirers but there was nothing she could do about that. It came with the territory of being in the public eye. People from all walks of life posted all sorts of comments on her Facebook fan page. Jameer checked the page frequently and always made a big deal about some of the comments that people posted.

In a television interview on a morning program a few months ago, the host had told Chasity that she made reading sexy. Jameer had argued with her for two days, accusing her of embarrassing him by flirting with the host on national television.

"Look Jameer...I need you to stop saying that. You know I'm not cheating on you. I just need some space to write, that's all. I'm having a difficult time lately and I'm trying to get my groove back. Why can't you understand that?"

"We'll talk when I get there. See you in a few minutes," Jameer responded and terminated the call.

Chasity turned back and took the bottle of wine from the refrigerator.

She was going to need more than one drink.

It was going to be a long night.

Chapter 23

Chasity opened the door to let Jameer in. He had arrived so quickly after hanging up the phone that she suspected he had been parked outside the complex when he called. He stepped in and Chasity closed the door.

"You don't look happy to see me," he said, pulling her close. He kissed her. She was unresponsive. His eyes narrowed.

"We really need to talk," Chasity said, extricating herself from his arms. He had been smoking. His new habit. She could smell the pungent odour of marijuana. She was no prude but she didn't like him smoking weed. He simply couldn't handle it and he was very aggressive when he was high.

She walked over to the couch and sat down. He came over and sat next to her. He started rubbing on her leg.

On second thought, maybe this wasn't a good time. It would not go well. It was obvious what he really came over for. He was horny. Having a serious conversation was the last thing on his mind.

He didn't even ask her what she wanted to talk about. He started nibbling on her neck and pushed his hand underneath her baby T. She wasn't wearing a bra. He groped her full breasts roughly.

Chasity sighed. She was not in the mood. All she wanted to do was think about her book and try to get the first paragraph started. But it was better to just go along with it than to try and get him to stop.

She allowed him to pull her shorts and panties off. She watched as he quickly shed his clothes. Jameer was 5' 10" and had a nice, sturdy build. She used to feel so safe in his strong arms. These days those strong arms scared her. He was getting unpredictable. His short fuse was even shorter, and he got angry over the silliest things. Jameer had slowly transformed from a mostly caring and considerate man to an insecure, whining, argumentative jerk.

They had met a few weeks before her first book was released and though she had liked him well enough, she wasn't really interested in a relationship. After her breakup with Chris, who had been her boyfriend since high school, she had decided to focus on her writing career. But Jameer stuck it out and eventually wore her down. They had now been serious for a year and a half. At the rate things were going, she doubted they would make it to the two year mark. Things would have to change.

"Jameer...stop...put a condom on," Chasity told him, closing her legs and preventing him from mounting her. They had stopped using condoms several months ago but she had decided to start using them again. Though she was on the pill, she could not be too careful. With the way Jameer had been acting in the past few months, getting pregnant for him at this juncture would be the worst possible scenario.

He frowned and looked at Chasity for several moments before he rummaged through his jeans' pocket and extracted one.

He rolled it on and pulled her to the edge of the sofa.

"Jameer...I'm not wet...eat me first, please."

"See...you don't even get excited for me anymore," he barked, his eyes, red from the effects of the marijuana he had smoked minutes before coming by, blazing with anger.

"Its not that...I'm just stressed that's all..." she said soothingly, trying to placate him. But he was right. Lately her sex drive was out of gas. And that was not typical. She loved sex. And she was a very passionate woman. She chalked it up to a combination of Jameer's disgusting behaviour and her writer's block.

Jameer gave her a look that suggested he believed otherwise but he sank to his knees and licked her long enough to get her sufficiently moist.

He then placed her legs on his shoulder and entered her with a firm thrust.

Chasity closed her eyes and prayed that he would climax quickly.

Chapter 24

Laku arrived at the Norman Manley International
Airport in Kingston at 11 p.m. He had taken a
flight to London and after a two hour wait at Heathrow,
got connected to his first class flight to Jamaica. The
pretty air hostess had flirted with him brazenly, and
Laku had joined the mile high club, giving the smittened
brunette a brief but satisfying thrill in the cramped
bathroom, stuffing her panties in her mouth to muffle
her cries of passion.

He retrieved his black six piece Vuitton luggage and
was the first one to reach the immigration officer. He
handed over his passport and three minutes later, with
a porter trailing him with his luggage, he made his way
to the exit.

Dressed in white fitted Dior slacks, a white Tom Ford
shirt with the sleeves rolled up to his elbows, reddish tint

Dolce & Gabbana glasses, and a pair of beige Gucci loafers, he was an arresting sight as he sauntered outside.

Fellow travelers and the people outside waiting for them stared at the handsome man and wondered who he was. The guesses ranged from movie star to rock star to fashion designer. Laku smiled inwardly as he casually read a few of their minds. The tall statuesque woman in all black who was standing with three other women was wondering why he didn't have an entourage. They didn't know he was but he must be *somebody*.

Laku spotted the man with the sign. It read LAKU. He walked over to him.

"I'm Laku."

"Welcome to Jamaica," the man said with a warmth and smile that the Jamaica Tourist Board would be proud of. "I am Tommy, your driver."

Once he decided he was going to Jamaica, Laku had looked up resorts on the internet and decided to choose a resort in San San, Portland. The place was secluded, luxurious and private, and the parish of Portland was generally rainy and cool. Perfect. He didn't come to Jamaica for the sun.

He had also rented a vehicle from the villa's fleet, a Mercedes truck which Tommy had driven to pick him up in. Tommy came with the truck but Laku would not need him after tonight. He would be driving himself around.

The porter loaded Laku's luggage in the metallic grey Mercedes G-class SUV. Laku tipped him twenty

Euros and climbed into the rear of the SUV. Tommy hopped in behind the wheel and they headed out.

Tommy was quite happy to entertain his quiet passenger with stories and a history lesson about Jamaica.

Laku listened absently as he looked out of the window.

The pictures were right.

Jamaica was indeed a beautiful country.

He was pleased that he came.

He had a strong feeling that it would be a memorable trip.

They arrived at the villa at 12:50 a.m. The property, called The Palms, was a visual feast located on a seven-acre buffet of lush land, nestled in the heart of the bush. Consisting of three self-contained state of the art two-bedroom villas and three deluxe cabins that all included a steam room, home theater, mini-bar, private outdoor veranda and lounge, wireless internet, private Jacuzzi, a personal chef available from 7 a.m. to midnight, twenty-four hour room service, secluded, unspoiled beaches and spectacular ocean and forest views.

Laku was met by Toi, the night manager, a lovely buxom woman with bright eyes and a ready smile. Her teeth were as white as chalk and were a stark contrast to her dark, smooth, mahogany skin.

She checked Laku in quickly and two minutes later, she escorted him along the softly lit, palm-tree lined stone path to his villa. A bell boy pushed his luggage on a trolley behind them. Laku read her thoughts on the walk over. She thought he was gay. He was too beautiful to be straight. Laku was amused at her logic. If he felt like it, perhaps later he would show her that she was wrong. He was so homophobic that he didn't even drink male blood.

"Here we are," Toi announced, when they got to the uber-luxurious villa. Laku gestured for the bell boy to leave his luggage at the door. "I do hope you enjoy your stay with us. Anything you need, all you have to do is call."

"Thank you." Laku fixed her with a penetrating stare and Toi wondered if her wet crotch was visible through her white pants. Sweet Jesus. Just one look and she was creaming her panties. It was extremely disconcerting.

"Ok, have a good night." Toi smiled and left. She was so wet that she wondered if the bell boy could hear a squishing sound as she walked. She would have to stay clear of this new guest. It was against company policy for anyone who worked there to fraternize with the guests.

Everything about him was just so seductive. The way he looked, the way he dressed, the way he spoke, the way he looked at her. She knew that she wouldn't stand a chance if she was alone with him. And that was scary. She didn't get down like that. She was not a promiscuous woman by any measure. She loved sex but within the confines of a relationship. It was beyond her comprehension how she could so easily see herself making love to a stranger.

Laku Leon.

She googled him as soon as she got back to her office.

Chapter 25

Laku unpacked some of his clothes and hung them in the large walk-in closet. He then took a quick shower and wearing a black and white striped Yves Saint Laurent robe, he went out to the private outdoor verandah. The Palms was truly a taste of paradise. Nature and luxury perfectly intertwined. It was a very expensive resort, but as far as Laku could see, it was worth every penny. This was a place for lovers. He thought of Franciska. She would have loved it here.

Laku brushed thoughts of Franciska aside and sank into one of the comfortable lounge chairs. He hummed a Chopin ballade as he powered up his iPad. His iPod aside, he wasn't very fond of gadgets but he loved to read and the iPad allowed him to store hundreds of books. Plus he could buy books from the Apple iBook store at any time. It didn't hurt that he could also surf the web, listen to music and watch a movie all in one go. Besides it was a beautiful device. And he was a lover of beautiful things.

He browsed his bookshelf but didn't see anything that matched his current mood. He wanted something romantic but dark and edgy. He checked the listings in the iBook store. After skimming through, he came upon a book that caught his eye. He liked the oxymoronic title. *The Flying Ostrich*. He read the blurb and the sample chapter provided. He was intrigued. He then read the author's bio and looked at her torso shot. She had on a white blouse with ruffles and Chanel reading glasses. She was very pretty, though she seemed oblivious of her beauty. Her soft and intelligent eyes looked directly into the camera, and her generous mouth, ripe with promise, pouted sexily, though Laku was positive that that was not her intention. There was an innocence about her that appealed to him.

Chasity Ray.

Laku liked her name.

He looked at her photo for a long time.

Then he purchased both of her novels, downloaded them, and began to read.

Toi said goodbye to the day manager, who came in to relieve her at 6:30 a.m., and inexplicably made her way over to the villa where Laku was staying, instead of heading to her car and going home. This type of unprofessional, reckless behaviour was totally uncharacteristic of her.

Laku had her in a trance. She had not stopped thinking about him since she checked him in. She had spent over an hour pouring over the information she had found on the web. Laku Leon was a revered French artist. He was regarded as a genius. There were glowing commentaries on his work from people she had never heard of but who were respected figures in the art world. Disappointedly, there was little personal information on the man himself. She had looked at photos of some of his paintings. She was no connoisseur of art, she couldn't tell the difference between a Renoir and a Warhol, but even to her unsophisticated eye, his paintings were exquisite. They were mesmerizing to look at.

She got to his villa and was about to knock when she heard a voice from inside tell her that it was open. She jumped in fright. How did he know that she was at his door? Trembling with anticipation, dripping with desire and ignoring her common sense, Toi went inside and closed the door behind her.

The windows were shut and the drapes closed. The only lighting in the living room came from an adjustable lamp that was shaped like a three-headed dragon. Laku was sitting on the leather love seat facing the door. He was wearing a robe but he might as well have been naked. Toi, her mouth slightly agape, leaned against the door for support. She could make out his ripped, firm chest and his proud erection, standing tall and rigid. He had known that she was coming. He was ready and waiting. How was that even possible?

She walked over to him slowly and stopped directly in front of him. She was putting her well-paying job that she loved so much in jeopardy. She was about to give her body to a man that she didn't know. Clearly she had lost her mind. She hoped that it was at least backed up on a disc somewhere.

"I've never done anything like this before," Toi whispered, as she dropped her pocketbook onto the carpeted floor.

Laku smiled indulgently, but did not respond.

Toi removed her blazer, which had the resort's name and logo on the top left, and as she anxiously shed the rest of her clothing, she was thankful that she had worn a matching set of underwear to work.

Naked in all her glory, her body a raging inferno, her mind a mass of confusion, lust and excitement, she stood nervously as he looked her over with an intense expression on his handsome face.

Toi was built like a brick house, and not one brick was missing. She had thick legs, a large firm ass, huge breasts, and wide child-bearing hips. It was a body designed for sinful activities. He was not used to women of this size, and this would be his first time with a black woman. It was well overdue. This was what his trip was all about. Experiencing new things and enjoying new delights.

"Touch yourself."

His command sent shivers down her spine and up her groin. She was incredibly wet. Her thighs were stained with her juices. Her right hand snaked down to the mass of prominent flesh between her legs and she cupped her mound, squeezing it gently before slipping two fingers inside. The heat that she felt made her gasp audibly. Her pussy felt as though it was literally on fire.

Groaning, she maintained eye contact with Laku as she worked her fingers in a seesaw motion, spreading her legs wider, hunching her back slightly as she felt her orgasm rushing to her center with alarming speed. She had only masturbated twice in her life and both times she had given up in frustration, unable to bring herself to a climax. Yet here she was, about to come so hard that she feared her usually sturdy legs would give way.

"Oh my God...ohhhh...I'm coming! I'm coming!" she shrieked, her hand a blur as she fingered herself rapidly. Her orgasm arrived and held her in an erotic choke-hold, making her croak and shudder uncontrollably, as her juices flowed freely down her legs.

Laku got up and Toi gasped as he lifted her one hundred and fifty pound frame effortlessly and brought her down onto his phallus. He pierced her easily, and her eyes rolled to the back of her head as he filled her up over and over again, plunging his rock hard flesh inside her with surgical precision as he walked around the villa with her, ending up in the kitchen. He placed her on the counter and continued to stoke her fire, his eyes blazing with unbridled passion. Toi's orgasms flowed into each other like she was chain-smoking and using one cigarette to light the other.

Toi ran her hands through his curly hair as she moaned like a wounded animal. Sex could not be this good. This intense. This mind-boggling. Everything was just so surreal. Surely she must be dreaming.

Her dream would last for another hour.

Chapter 26

Laku flicked through the many available channels and eventually settled on an action movie about a bank robbery gone awry. Toi had left to go home a little over an hour ago. He had enjoyed having sex with her, though the entire time he had been thinking about the romance novelist. Chasity Ray. He had enjoyed her books. She was a very good writer. Quirky and unique. He simply could not stop thinking about her. The last time a woman had affected him like this it had changed his life forever.

The Jamaica Booksellers and Publishers Association were having an awards ceremony tomorrow evening at 7:00 p.m. She was up for two awards. Her sophomore novel, *Life Interrupted,* was nominated for Best Adult Creative Writing and Best Adult Fiction Cover. Chasity had posted the information on her Facebook fanpage which Laku had spent a long time going through, looking at pictures and reading the comments from her fans.

There was no question about it.

He simply had to meet her.

He would be going to Kingston tonight.

He had already gone online and booked a suite at the Danish Court Hotel.

He would drive there at dusk.

Toi woke up at 5:30 p.m. She looked at the clock in amazement and jumped out of bed. She had slept the entire day. After getting home a few minutes past 8, she had showered and went straight to bed, and was just now waking up. She yawned as she made her way to the bathroom to take a quick shower. She needed to get ready for work. She had missed Merrick, her live-in boyfriend this morning as she got home after he had already left for work, and she would miss him this evening as she would be gone by the time he got home.

She was grateful for that as she needed time to gather her thoughts. It was the first time that she had cheated on him in their three year old relationship and though she did feel a tad bit guilty, she would do it again if given the chance. She could never regret anything that had given her such immense pleasure. And to think that she had thought Laku was a homosexual. The joke was on her. It had been the most magical experience of her life. Laku had to be the most virile man on the planet. And the strangest too. He was unlike anyone that she had ever met. Mysterious and intriguing. Dangerous even. She had felt so many different emotions and vibes during her time with him.

She stepped into the shower and turned the water on. She was so hungry that she felt light-headed. Laku had drained her body of its precious nutrients. She would have dinner at the hotel.

She showered quickly and half an hour later, she was on her way to work.

She got there in twelve minutes.

She buzzed the chef immediately.

Laku enjoyed the sounds of The Velvet Underground as he drove past the sign that read WELCOME TO THE PARISH OF ST. THOMAS. He had left the lush parish of Portland behind and was now only an hour away from Kingston. He was enjoying the drive.

He had plugged his iPod into the SUV's Bose speakers, giving him full access to his favourite albums for the long ride. He recalled some of the things that Tommy had told him about St. Thomas when they passed through on their way to Portland from the airport. It was Jamaica's ninth largest parish, very mountainous, and had three main rivers including the

Plantation Garden River, which was the only river in the island to flow eastward. According to Tommy, St. Thomas also had a very high number of obeah men who practiced witchcraft. People came to see them from far and wide to ward off bad luck or to put a spell on their enemies. Laku wondered wryly what a so-called obeah man would do if he came across a vampire.

As he passed through the town of Yallahs, it began to rain. Heavily. Huge hail-like raindrops pelted the luxury SUV angrily. It was a sudden downpour. He could see pedestrians scurrying for cover.

He wondered what Chasity was doing at this moment.

He wondered if she had a premonition that her life was about to change.

He wasn't sure what was going to happen when they met, but one way or another, her life would never be the same.

Toi was not having a good night at work. She had learnt that Laku was gone and would be away for a few days. He had left instructions that his villa was not to be cleaned. No one was to go inside there while he was away. She wondered where he had gone and how long he would be away. Though it wasn't a certainty that he would have wanted to see her when she got off work, it would have been a possibility. He consumed her thoughts. She could think of nothing but her experience with him. It had been out of this world and she wanted more. He was like a drug. One taste and she was addicted. Laku had booked the villa for two weeks. He would be going back to France two days after Christmas.

She wondered if he would keep in touch after he left. Allow her to visit him in France. That would be so romantic. She knew that she was getting ahead of herself but a girl could dream, couldn't she?

She snapped out of her reverie when a guest entered the lobby, laughing raucously. It was the big time record producer from the UK. He was with two women. He was a very demanding guest and his ego was bigger than his stomach, which was a remarkable feat.

She summoned a warm smile and tried to push Laku to the recesses of her mind.

"No, I can't. You know I'm having cocktails with Sabrina tonight," Chasity told Jameer as she applied the finishing touches to her make-up. He had called wanting to take her out to celebrate her nomination for the two JBAPA awards despite the fact that he knew she would be hanging out with her best friend tonight.

"Ok...so where you guys going?" Jameer asked after a pregnant pause.

"I don't know yet," Chasity lied. They would be going to the poolside bar at the Danish Court Hotel. It was Kingston's latest trendy spot for cocktails. But she didn't want Jameer to know that as she was sure that he would show up there. He had done it before a couple of weeks ago when she was having a business dinner with a client and embarrassed her by creating a scene. She just couldn't understand how Jameer had transformed into this needy, insecure man who didn't want her to do anything without him. It was seriously getting to her. She had tried talking to him about it the other day and he had trivialized her concerns by saying that she was overreacting.

"Call me when you get home," he said, and ended the call.

Chasity placed the phone down on the dresser and applied her lipstick. She was a very patient, laidback woman that hated confrontation but everyone had a breaking point and Lord knows she was very close to hers. She gave herself a final onceover in the mirror and pleased with what she saw, retrieved her pocketbook and headed out. She deliberately left her cell phone. Despite asking her to call him when she got home, she knew that Jameer would still call while she was out.

She glanced at the time. It was 8:05 p.m. She was supposed to meet Sabrina at 8:15 by the bar. She would get there on time. She only lived ten minutes away, less if there wasn't much traffic.

She hopped into her black Honda Accord coupe and headed out.

Laku was in high spirits as he turned onto Knutsford Boulevard and was greeted by the modern metropolis that was New Kingston. He glanced at the imposing sculpture of a naked couple looking skyward as he drove past Emancipation Park, one of New Kingston's landmarks. He could feel the pulse of the city as he drove along the bustling hip strip, passing nightclubs, fine restaurants, multi-storied office buildings, stores and banks. The place had a very different vibe from the laidback, tourist feel of Portland. It had the energy and charged air of excitement that all major cities should have.

He turned onto St. Vincent Avenue and was soon at the entrance of the Danish Court Hotel. Finding the place was a breeze, thanks to the map on his iPad and his keen sense of direction. After a quick, polite query from the uniformed guard at the gate, he drove in and pulled up in front of the lobby behind a gleaming white BMW convertible. He handed the valet his keys and a porter followed with his two pieces of luggage as he strutted inside.

The spacious lobby was very modern and tastefully decorated with exquisitely designed chairs, created by a Jamaican designer of international repute, and a revolving collection of black and white prints from world renowned photographers. A café also called the lobby home, serving Continental and Jamaican cuisine, as well as a gourmet selection of desserts, tea and coffee.

Five minutes later he was on an elevator heading to his penthouse suite on the fourth floor. The hotel was more sprawling than high, and only had four floors.

Laku tipped the porter twenty Euros, who thanked him profusely, and made a mental note to get some Jamaican currency. He looked around the suite and considered it suitable for his tastes. There was a King-sized bed, air conditioner and ceiling fan, a 42 inch Plasma flat screen, an iPod dock, a mini bar, black out blinds and an oval shaped soaking tub and shower. Wireless internet was available in the room and throughout the property.

Laku looked over his clothing and satisfied that he didn't need to change - he was wearing a black V neck T-shirt underneath a fitted black blazer with the sleeves pulled up to the elbows, black Dior jeans and a pair of wine red Prada loafers – he made his way downstairs.

He certainly didn't come to Kingston to stay inside his suite.

Chapter 27

"I'm so proud of you Chas," Sabrina said. She raised her glass of red wine in a toast. "Here's to your continued success."

"Thanks Brina." Chasity smiled as they clinked their glasses lightly and drank to her success. She didn't have many close friends and was thankful whenever Sabrina's schedule allowed her to be in Jamaica. Sabrina was a track and field athlete who specialized in the 100m hurdles. She had her best season ever on the circuit this year, posting a new personal best and beating the current World and Olympic champion at a meet in Brussels. She had gotten a new coach eighteen months ago and was now seeing excellent results. She was looking forward to the World Championships next year, where she hoped to get a medal.

Sabrina and Chasity had been friends since the

tenth grade. Talented and ambitious, both of them had been popular students despite their quiet, laidback personalities. Sabrina had been a star athlete, representing their school admirably for several years at the National Girl's Championships and held the school record for the 100m hurdles. Chasity had entered and won several national writing competitions, bringing the school much acclaim in the arts.

After high school Sabrina went away to Texas A&M University on an athletic scholarship while Chasity stayed in Jamaica and attended the University of the Visual Arts. They had stayed in constant touch and visited each other whenever possible.

"So what are you going to do about Jameer?" Sabrina asked, her light brown eyes now serious. Chasity had confided in her about Jameer's behaviour and she was very upset about it. She had never liked him and always thought that Chasity could do so much better. She was not too surprised that he was now showing his true colours. He had always struck her as a weakling and a fake. What kind of man was jealous of his woman's success? Only a real loser as far as she was concerned.

Chasity sighed. She had only just recently told Sabrina about the situation. She knew that Sabrina didn't like Jameer. She really did need to do something. She hadn't told Sabrina the entire story. She was too embarrassed to admit that she was afraid of Jameer. The way things were going it was just a matter of time before he hurt her physically.

"Damn! Who is *that?*" Sabrina said, interrupting her thoughts.

Chasity followed Sabrina's eyes and her heart skipped several beats.

It could not be possible.

It was the guy that she had dreamt about last night.

Laku sauntered to the bar, feeling many eyes on him, hearing many thoughts. He slid into an empty chair close to the end of the circular bar, and ordered a drink of Remy Martin. He looked around as the bartender poured his drink and their eyes connected.

Chasity Ray.

She was looking at him like she had seen a ghost.

He had tapped into her energy and appeared to her last night. She thought it was a dream. But it was a vision. He had showed her the things that he was going to do to her. The pleasures he would bring her.

She was even more beautiful in person. Flawless make-up that emphasized her natural beauty. Full lips covered by trendy neon pink Mac lip stick. Long, toned legs cased in black leggings. Her hair was different from the pictures on her Facebook fan page. It was now

shoulder length on the right side and closely cropped
on the left. A stylish nerd. That's the term that came
to Laku's mind. She was captivating. She was reliving
the dream. Her face was flushed and she was unable to
look away from him.

Laku smiled and turned back around. He took a sip
of his drink that the bartender had placed in front of
him.

"Chas...are you ok?" Sabrina asked. Chasity had a
really strange look on her face. "Do you know him?"

"Yes, I mean no," she blabbered. "This is unreal."

Sabrina was looking at her like she was going crazy.
She probably was. She took a sip of her wine to calm
her nerves. It didn't work. She had not thought about
the dream all day. She had actually forgotten about it
when she woke up, and had frowned in surprise at the
residue left in her panties from her secretions. Seeing
him had sharply brought back the memory of it. It had
been so passionate, so intense, so real, so exhilarating.
She remembered his body. Hard like marble and perfectly
sculpted like a Roman statue. She remembered how he
felt inside her. Hard, thick and long. Stroking her like
he had designed her anatomy. She remembered his
touch. Cold hands, tongue and lips that roamed every
crevice and curve of her body, uncovering erotic secrets,

turning her into molten lava. Setting her soul on fire. She had climaxed over and over and over again. Something she rarely did in real life. Orgasms were as common for her as finding a hundred dollar bill on the street.

But this wasn't a dream.

He was here in real life.

And he was sitting less than a hundred feet away.

Chapter 28

"**O**ut with it Chas...the suspense is killing me!" Sabrina beseeched, anxiously leaning closer to Chasity.

Chasity sighed. "This is kind of embarrassing..."

Sabrina rolled her eyes impatiently. "I'm your best friend...I know your most embarrassing moments... stop hedging."

"Ok, ok. I had a really erotic dream last night..." She paused and looked over at the bar. The guy's back was to them, and he was in a conversation with a slender, busty Caucasian woman, who seemed to be a business-woman, based on her attire, knocking back a few drinks. The woman laughed at something he said and lightly touched his arm. Chasity felt a pang of jealousy and immediately got upset with herself for having such a reaction. She didn't even know this man!

"And he's the guy that was making love to me..." Chasity continued. "He looks exactly the same, down to his red contacts."

"Wow...that's some freaky shit," Sabrina cackled. "So was it good?"

Chasity emitted a long sigh. "Girl, it was out of this world. I came so many times I lost count."

Sabrina laughed heartily. "That was some dream. Really weird though."

They were silent for a few moments, wrapped inside their own thoughts.

"He's the hottest man I've seen in a long time," Sabrina commented wistfully.

Chasity looked at her sharply.

Don't even think about it. He's mine!

"Well excuse me Miss Thing...you forget that you have a boyfriend?"

Chasity's mouth became a wide O. She couldn't believe that she had said that out loud.

What the hell was happening to her?

She took a hearty sip of her wine, and then stared at the glass, as though the answer lied in it.

An hour and a half and three glasses of red wine later, Chasity decided to call it a night. The object of her intrigue had left about an hour ago, in the company of the woman, much to her chagrin. It had inexplicably but positively ruined her night.

"I really wish I could be there tomorrow to see you collect your awards," Sabrina said as they walked out to the cobblestone parking lot. She had to go back to Florida tomorrow morning to fulfill an obligation with Adidas, her sponsor.

"Its ok hun, I know you have your business to take care of. I'll email the pictures."

"I leave really early so I won't call until about midday," Sabrina told her.

They hugged tightly and went to their vehicles. Sabrina had borrowed her mother's Toyota Camry.

Chasity was deep in thought as she reached her vehicle and deactivated the alarm. She wasn't aware of his presence until he spoke.

"Bonjour jolie dame."

She jumped in fright and dropped her keys. She wasn't sure what he just said but she thought a hello was in there somewhere. His voice was something out of a dream. Melodic, soothing, seductive and entirely masculine. It gave her goose pimples.

"Hi, you startled me. Do you always sneak up on poor defenseless women like that?"

"Mes excuses."

He picked up her keys and handed them to her, then extended his right hand. "I'm Laku."

She shook it and was shocked at its coldness. Even more shocking was the heat-wave it sent through her entire frame. "I'm Chasity."

He stared at her intently.

She squirmed underneath his penetrating gaze.

"Your contacts are very unusual," she said, breaking the silence that had gotten way too intense for her liking.

"They're not contacts," he responded, undressing her with the eyes in question. "That's how my eyes are."

"Really? Wow...they're fascinating." She could only imagine how many panties those eyes and handsome features had caused to drop much more quickly than the owners would have liked.

"Thank you."

She was acutely aware that they were still holding hands and she had no desire to remove hers.

Laku pulled her against him suddenly.

She gasped, and was immediately cognizant of his ridiculously hard body pressed against hers. Her pussy began to behave inappropriately. It became extremely hot and wet, like it had a high fever.

"I have a confession," he said softly.

Chasity didn't trust herself to speak. Her pretty brown eyes regarded him in confused contentment. She didn't understand all the emotions that this complete stranger had invoked in her, but there was nowhere else she would rather be than in his arms. This was utter madness. Something out of the pages of one her novels. But then again, as she always quoted, her art didn't imitate life, it was life.

"I know who you are...and I have read your two novels. They were very good."

The surprise showed on her face. He had read her books! And he had enjoyed them. She was extremely pleased. She was always humbled when people told her how much they enjoyed her work but this compliment inexplicably meant more to her than any she had ever received. She couldn't understand why.

"Thank you." Her voice was a hoarse whisper.

"I really liked Elle. A very deep character. I see a lot of you in her. She is you, without restraint."

Chasity's jaws dropped. Elle was the heroine of *Life Interrupted*. Elle was her. Elle was who she would be if she fully immersed herself in her art and worried less about being conventional and playing by life's rules. If she didn't give a damn about what people thought of her. Elle was true freedom. Elle lived life without fear, viewing the world through 3D lenses. There was never a dull moment in Elle's world. In light of the fact that he didn't know her, it was amazing for him to be able to perceive that the character represented what she saw as her deepest inadequacies.

"I don't know what to say...how did-" She trailed off in mid-sentence, feeling unusually inarticulate.

"Would you like to come up to my suite? We can have a drink and talk as we watch the stars from the balcony."

Chasity nodded and activated the alarm on her car.

As they walked towards the lobby, still holding hands, Chasity wondered how in the world it could be possible for her to be so completely comfortable with a total stranger.

Truth was indeed stranger than fiction.

Chapter 29

Jameer reversed from the gate and parked close to the entrance of the apartment complex where Chasity lived. He was seething with rage. He had been calling her for the past hour, left six messages on her voicemail and sent her three texts, and she had yet to respond. He had driven over to her complex, only to be told by the new guard at the gate that Ms. Ray was not home and as such he could not allow him inside the complex to wait until she got home. Fucking prick.

This had confirmed his fears. Chasity was cheating on him. She had lied about hanging out with Sabrina and not knowing where they'd be hanging out. She was with a man. Why else would she be ignoring his calls and texts for such a long period of time? And why wasn't she back home yet? She had been gone for close to three hours.

He was not going to tolerate this kind of disrespect. She was going to pay, and pay dearly. Maybe she thought that because she had a few fans and got nominated for a couple of awards that she was a big star and could treat him any way she desired. Well he had news for her. That most certainly was not the case. When he got through with her she'd be lucky if she could even attend the awards show.

He lit the marijuana joint that he had just rolled and took a deep drag.

A police car on patrol in the area drove past the parked car slowly, and stopped alongside it when they realized that someone was in it. A cloud of smoke had just been blown out of the car.

"What's that you're smoking...doesn't smell like a cigarette," the cop in the passenger seat said, his pimple-riddled face deadly serious.

Jameer groaned inwardly. Just what he needed. A couple of cops with nothing better to do busting his chops over a simple joint. He forced a disarming smile.

"Just a little spliff officer...can't get in touch with my girl and it's stressing me out."

"Come out of the car with your licenses and registration," the officer said sternly as he stepped out of the police car.

Jameer shook his head in frustration and retrieved the documents for his car from the glove compartment, and fished his driver's license from out of his wallet. He stepped out of the car and handed them to the cop.

He stubbed out the marijuana joint but did not throw it away.

The cop examined the documents and handed them back to him. He looked at the license and then looked at the Jameer.

"I'm sure you know it's against the law to smoke marijuana Mr. Gunther. We're going to have to take you in for illegal possession of marijuana."

"Officer, please, don't bother with that man, its just one little spliff," Jameer begged. If they locked him up tonight he wouldn't be able to get bail until Monday morning. He would spend the rest of the weekend in lock-up and that was a terrifying prospect.

"Well, what can you do to convince me to give you a chance?"

Jameer breathed easier. The cop would accept a bribe.

"Can give you a t'ing," Jameer said, thanking his lucky stars that he had his ATM card with him.

The cop looked at him for a few minutes before responding.

"Ok, what you have?" he finally said.

Jameer thought quickly. If he offered too little a sum the cop would be insulted and still might arrest him but at the same time he didn't want to give them more than he had to.

"I can give you seven thousand," Jameer told him, praying that he would accept.

"Make it ten," the cop countered.

Jameer nodded and told them he had to go an ATM machine.

The cops drove behind him to Oxford Road at the Texaco gas station where the closest ATM machine was located.

Jameer withdrew the cash, cursing his luck but grateful that he would not be going to jail. He handed the cop the money and they drove away quickly.

Jameer got into his car and slammed the door. He pounded the steering wheel in frustration and anger.

This was all Chasity's fault.

God help her when he got his hands on her.

"I'd love to see your work," Chasity purred, the wine and chocolate making her feel extremely relaxed and mellow. They were on the bedroom balcony of Laku's suite, enjoying an exquisite bottle of white wine that Laku had ordered through room service and delightful handmade gourmet chocolate that she had all to herself, as Laku said he was not hungry.

Laku got up and went to fetch his iPad. The night was going well. He now understood why he was so drawn to her. Chasity was a rare breed. Unpretentious, smart, artistic, beautiful, talented and sexy. He was thoroughly enjoying her company. It was the first time since Franciska that he was having interest in a woman, other than to feed on or to have sex with. He enjoyed talking to her, hearing her opinions about anything, from Lebron James leaving Cleveland to play for Miami, to Obama's performance as President, to global warming, to love.

He returned to the balcony and sat beside her. She drew closer to him as he powered up the iPad. He breathed in her scent. She smelled so good. He could only imagine how sweet her blood would taste, satisfying his thirst as he drank with unbridled gusto. He imagined how good it would feel to make love to her supple body, making her lose control and scream his name over and over again as he plunged deeply inside her, filling her with hardened ecstasy, wrenching orgasms from deep inside her soul, taking her to places where only true lovers could go.

Laku did a Google search on his name and handed her the device. Chasity scrolled through, looking at him in amazement as she checked the articles written about his work and looked at pictures of some of his paintings.

"Oh my God...you're absolutely brilliant. I'm in the presence of Art royalty," she said half-jokingly.

Laku smiled at her, and brushed her left cheek with the faintest of touches. Chasity melted. She couldn't take it anymore. She placed the iPad on the extra chair beside her and climbed onto Laku's lap. She couldn't believe that this was her in action.

Dear God, what has this magnificent man done to me?

Laku looked at her, his brilliant red eyes brimming with lust and desire. Chasity moaned and lowered her head, claiming his lips with an unfamiliar hunger. Her eyes tightly shut, she cupped his cold cheeks with both hands as she kissed him deeply and passionately, exploring his sweet mouth with wild abandon.

Laku eased her dress up around her waist and reached down with his right hand and pulled her thong to the side. He placed his hand between her legs and massaged her shaven mound. Chasity's eyes fluttered open as he slid a solitary finger inside her hot core.

"Oh my God...mmmm...that feels so good..." Chasity moaned, finally breaking their searing kiss. Her lips remained inches from his as he stroked her with his finger, relishing the way her sugar walls closed in on his finger as it slid back and forth. She was tight. He could only imagine how she would choke his shaft when he went inside her.

Chasity clutched Laku tightly as she felt a tingle in the center of her heat. He was going to make her come. She was going to drown his finger. Her body tensed in anticipation. She gasped and shuddered as pleasure coursed through her veins.

Laku gestured for her to rise. She got up from off his lap, holding onto his broad shoulders for support. Her legs were currently about as firm as water. Laku unbuttoned his jeans and pulled them to his ankles along with his boxers.

"Sweet Jesus..." Chasity croaked when she reached down to guide his shaft inside her. It was the hardest piece of flesh she had ever touched in her life. She wondered if she would be able to comfortably accommodate him. He was offering way more than she was used to.

She lowered herself slowly, maintaining eye contact with Laku as he pierced her saturated flesh, groaning loudly as he filled her to capacity. Her breathing erratic, she sat on it without moving, acclimatizing herself to the unfamiliar feel of having such a huge appendage inside her.

Chasity emitted unfeminine grunts as she began to slowly bounce on his shaft, savouring the new exquisite pleasures and relishing the new sensations that Laku was introducing her to. She began to move faster, groan louder. The sane part of her wondered if anyone could see or hear them. Wondered what she was doing having unprotected sex with a man she just met mere hours ago.

The unleashed, adventurous part of her drowned out the naysayer. The higher she soared, the closer to the clouds she got, the more the voice of reason faded, until she could hear it no more. This side wasn't shackled by conventional wisdom.

This side didn't give a damn.

She was completely immersed in the moment, screaming out Laku's name as she climaxed hard, her body shaking violently as she reached heights of pleasure that she didn't know existed.

"*Tu es si belle,*" Laku murmured, giving her a look that made her feel like the most desirable woman in the world.

Be careful Laku...you're going to make me fall in love with you.

Still deep inside her, Laku stood and shuffled into the bedroom, his pants and boxers still around his ankles.

He then lifted her from off his dick and made her stand. Without warning, Laku ripped her dress from off her body, tossing the ruined garment in the air. It landed on the ceiling fan and stayed there. Her underwear received the same treatment. His clothing quickly followed and in an instant they were on the bed, Chasity's legs on his shoulders as he plunged inside her relentlessly.

Chasity's head was spinning. Her heart was racing. Her breasts were heaving. Her pussy was pulsing. His sudden aggression had both scared and turned her on at the same time. Laku was taking her deep inside an erotic abyss where the pleasure was so intense it bordered on the insane.

It was exactly as it had been in her dream.

He was fucking her like he owned her mind, body and soul.

Chasity knew that after tonight she would never be the same.

Chapter 30

C hasity opened her eyes. No, she was not dreaming.
She was lying on Laku's chest, in his King-sized
bed at a penthouse suite at the Danish Court Hotel.
The memory of last night played in her mind, reel after
reel, like an erotic film. She blushed fiercely as she
remembered her wanton behaviour. She raised her head
and looked up at him. He was watching her. He smiled.

"*Bonjour*...did you sleep well?"

Chasity returned his smile and nodded. She couldn't
tell the last time that she had slept so soundly. She
had been utterly exhausted and completely sated after
the mind blowing sex they'd had.

She sat up slowly.

"Last night was incredible...in every way." She paused
and looked at him shyly. "I've never done anything like
that before...I hope you don't think badly of me."

Laku smiled at her reassuringly. "On the contrary, I am honoured that you shared yourself with me. Trust me…I'm fully aware of how special you are *Cherie*."

She basked in his words for a few moments.

"I need to take a shower," she said, and rose from the bed gingerly. She was pleasantly sore. She padded to the bathroom and closed the door behind her.

She gasped when she looked at her body in the full length mirror. She had love bites all over her body. They were huge and practically hurt when she touched them. It was a wonder he hadn't drawn blood.

She put on the shower cap that was available and climbed into the shower. She sighed contentedly as she turned on the warm water. She was feeling so *alive*. So *inspired*. So excited. After breakfast she would head home and do some writing. The book was calling her. Laku had cured her writer's block.

She smiled as she lathered herself with the shower gel.

Laku had turned her universe inside out.

And she loved it.

Maybe even loved him.

But she wasn't ready to think about that yet.

The idea of that was simply too crazy to absorb right now.

Laku listened to her thoughts as she showered. She was in love with him, though she had yet to admit it to herself. He needed to address his own feelings. Though he had been very drawn to her just by looking at her pictures and reading her work, he had not expected to enjoy being with her so much. Though the situation was different, on a completely emotive level, it rivaled what he had felt for Franciska. That was scary. He remembered the pain he had felt when Franciska betrayed his love, their love. And as an artist who processed pain the same way he processed pleasure, the pain had been atrocious. It was not an experience he would like to repeat, or cause someone to go through. It was foolhardy for him to reciprocate her feelings for him. What good could come of it? He was a vampire. What would she do if she found out? How would she feel about him then? Killing her was not an option. He would never do that, could never do that. Last night as he ravaged her body, nibbling on her, sucking all over her skin, he had never craved a human's blood so badly, yet he had not yielded to the unbearable temptation. That proved to him how much he cared about her.

He had just under two weeks left in Jamaica.

Soon he would have to make a serious decision where Chasity was concerned.

He would have to tell her he who really was and let the chips fall where they may, or he would have to vanish from her life forever, breaking her heart in the process.

He got out of bed and went to join her in the shower.

Thinking about her had given him a turgid erection.

Chapter 31

Chasity hummed the hook to Eminem's Rhianna assisted hit single *Love the Way You Lie* as she turned onto Kensington Crescent. She was feeling exuberant. On top of the world. It was now 11:30 a.m. After Laku surprised her in the shower and made her temporarily forget her hunger, they had breakfast in the suite brought up by room service – well she did, Laku inexplicably wasn't hungry – and then she had reluctantly left to go home. It was amazing how attached she was to him already. Though she was itching to go home and write, she did not want to leave him.

She was wearing one of his fitted button-downs as her dress, a cute little backless Calvin Klein number that she had picked up in Florida the last time she went there to visit Sabrina, had been torn to shreds. He promised to replace it.

She had invited him to escort her to the awards show. There was only one problem. Jameer was to have taken her. She had not thought about him the entire time she was with Laku. And that was telling. If she had really loved him there was no way she would feel so guiltless about what she had done. She now had the strength to do what she was supposed to have done at least four months ago.

It was over. Now it was just a matter of letting him know. She would not be able to tell him in person. There was no way she could do it while they were alone as she feared that he would physically attack her, and she couldn't do it in a public place as he would definitely create a big scene. She would have to call him and tell him.

As she opened the gate with her remote gate opener, she was suddenly aware of a car behind her. It was Jameer. He must have been parked outside of the complex waiting on her. She had been too engrossed in her thoughts to notice.

She put her window down.

"Don't let that guy in! I don't want to see him!" she said frantically to the security guard at the booth.

The guard looked at the vehicle behind her and frowned. It was the same guy from last night. Probably a crazy ex or something. He nodded at Chasity and stepped in front of Jameer's car, holding up his right hand while resting the left on the firearm on his side.

Chasity could see the crazed look on Jameer's face through her rear-view mirror. He looked like he wanted to kill somebody. And that somebody was her. She had seen him angry many times but never to that extent. She shuddered and drove in quickly. She parked in her spot and after a quick glance at the gate, headed inside and locked the door. She rummaged through the phone book, picked up the phone and dialed the number for the Danish Court Hotel.

Laku was not surprised when the phone in his suite rang. He had felt the sudden, drastic shift in her energy. She was anxious and afraid.

"What's wrong Chasity?" he asked without preamble.

How did he know it was me? Chasity wondered.

"It's my boy – well my ex-boyfriend Jameer, though he doesn't know it yet – I'm not making any sense... I'm sorry –"

"Shhh....relax and take a deep breath," Laku said soothingly.

She did as he suggested and it actually worked. Or maybe it was the sound of his voice. Whatever it was she was feeling much calmer now.

"Ok. Now tell me everything."

She did, all of it.

Laku listened intently.

He did not like what he was hearing.

After arguing with the security guard, who threatened to call the police if he didn't move away from the gate, Jameer drove away, not wanting to get entangled with the law. He was beyond furious. If the security guard wasn't carrying a gun he probably would have attacked him. Seeing Chasity drive in and go into her apartment and being unable to do anything about it had made him so angry it brought tears to his eyes. He had been waiting outside of the complex since 7 a.m. and had called her mobile ten times.

Where the hell was she coming from at this hour? A man's house, that's where. Jameer pulled over and banged on the dashboard with his fists. She was cheating on him and didn't even have the decency to hide it. She didn't care. She didn't give a damn about his feelings. She was even wearing the man's shirt. She probably reeked of sex. Slut! He couldn't wait to get his hands on her. He had never felt so disrespected in his life. His friends always teased him that he had overachieved when he snagged Chasity as his girl. "She'll soon wise up and leave you" Mark would often joke around the pool table.

He used to laugh and brush their comments off, but they had pierced him deeply. He would remember his mother's comments to him when he was growing up. *You won't come to anything. No good woman is going to want you. You're going to be a damn worthless drunk like your daddy.* His mother hated him. He was the splitting image of his father, a man his mother hated so much for leaving her that she prayed for his death frequently. When he was two years old his father had left to go to the bar to have a drink with his friends and he never came back. So she hated him too. He reminded her too much of his dad. He had not seen or spoken to her in six years.

Jameer's jaw was so tightly clenched that it was hurting. But it was nothing compared to the pain that he was feeling inside. He loved Chasity so much. He had felt her slipping away, and the more he tried to fix it, the worse things became. He emitted a tortured sigh. He was going to be a laughing scorn when his friends found out what happened. He would have to fix things. Right the ship.

She had hurt him deeply.

He was going repay that hurt twofold, but things would work out eventually. It had to. She could not leave him. She belonged to him. They belonged together.

She had lost her way but he would help her to find it.

By whatever means necessary.

Chapter 32

Laku saw the grey Acura ahead, parked at the curb a few feet away from the entrance to Chasity's complex. Jameer. Chasity was worried that he would cause trouble when she was leaving to go to the awards ceremony. She was right. There he was, waiting for her to leave. Laku could have easily drove in and picked her up and Jameer wouldn't be none the wiser, as he didn't know Laku and the Mercedes SUV was tinted.

But Laku was having none of that.

This was a problem and it needed to be addressed. Now.

He pulled up behind the car, parked and got out.

Laku walked over to Jameer's car. Jameer was sitting there, deep in thought, toying with a lighter in his right

155

hand. The window was down. Laku reached in with one hand, clutched Jameer firmly around the throat, and pulled a surprised Jameer through the window unceremoniously.

Jameer could barely breathe, much less speak. His eyes bulged in terror and confusion. Who the hell was this guy? Why was he doing this? How the hell was he so damn strong? Jameer was 5' 10" and had a stocky build. He worked out four times a week religiously at the gym where he was one of the instructors. Yet this stranger had pulled him from the car like he was a baby, and was now holding him up in the air, still with one hand, without breaking a sweat.

Jameer struggled, trying to break Laku's ice-cold vice grip on his neck. He was going to die. He couldn't breathe. His life flashed before his eyes. It surprised him that his happiest memory was when Chasity had agreed to be his girlfriend. Twenty-six years on the earth and that was his happiest memory. That was pitiful. His life was a waste. And now it was over.

Laku released him suddenly and he tumbled to the ground in a heap. He gasped and wheezed as his lungs gratefully gulped air. Laku looked down at him impassively. Jameer was a scruffy pathetic weasel. He couldn't imagine what Chasity had seen in him. But everyone was entitled to make mistakes.

Laku could smell his fear. Fear that had made him lose control of his bladder.

"If you ever contact Chasity again in any kind of way, I'm going to hunt you down and kill you."

Jameer's head snapped up, his eyes wide with surprise, before narrowing with painful understanding. Thinking something to be true and knowing it to be a fact were two completely different things. Though he had been certain that Chasity was cheating on him, there had been a glimmer of hope that he was wrong. The strange foreigner standing over him had snuffed out that hope.

So this was the man that had destroyed his happy relationship. That had taken his woman away from him. He was admittedly an extremely handsome and well-dressed man. He had an air of sophistication and confidence that people born into money tended to have. Jameer's ego, what was left of it, shriveled to the size of a peanut. He knew without a doubt that Chasity was lost to him to forever. This guy was playing in another league.

He looked into Laku's impossibly red eyes. It was like staring into the depths of hell. He cringed but could not look away. He was convinced that this man was a demon. How else could his eyes be so red and disturbing? How could he be so strong? His hands so hard and cold? Jameer's imagination ran rampant, filling him with stark terror. He could see the man snarling, fangs bared as he took a hold of him and ripped his head from his body as easily one would rip the wrapper from a candy bar.

His bowels loosened. A scream was inside him dying to come out but it was stuck in his throat. Jameer wanted nothing more than to get away from this man. He found himself praying, something he hadn't done in many years.

Laku looked at him contemptuously before walking away, satisfied that Jameer had gotten the message. He hopped into the rented SUV and drove off, turning into the entrance. The security guard, having been informed that Chasity was expecting a guest in a metallic grey Mercedes SUV between 7:30 and 7:45, opened the gate without query.

Laku drove in and pulled up at Apartment 3A, parking behind Chasity's Honda Accord. Having seen him drive in from her balcony, Chasity went back into the bedroom and looked at herself in the full length mirror. Pleased with what she saw, she turned off the light and headed out.

Laku had gotten out of the vehicle and was walking towards her front door when it opened. Chasity smiled at him and locked the door. Laku watched her as she approached him.

"*Vous regardez absolument magnifique.*"

"Thank you," Chasity said, as she hugged him. "Though I don't know what that means I'm sure it was a compliment."

Laku chuckled. "I said...you look absolutely beautiful."

Chasity blushed as she stood there in his arms. Laku had this way of looking at her that made her weak every single time. Made her believe that the words that came out of his mouth were true.

He led her by hand to the passenger side, opened the door and helped her in. Murmuring her thanks, and feeling like a princess, she sat down and Laku closed the door. He went around to the driver's side, got in and they headed out. Chasity became anxious as they drove through the gate.

"I took care of it. He won't bother you anymore," Laku told her without looking at her.

Chasity looked at his side profile as they headed down the street. A tidal wave of affection washed up on the shore of her heart and drenched the sands of her soul. She reached over and touched his cheek. It was cold, as usual. Yet his touch electrified her, as always.

They say that no one is perfect but Laku posed a serious challenge to that argument. She had yet to find a flaw. There had to be, of course, but whatever it was she was positive that it couldn't be too bad. As far as she was concerned, he was perfect for her. They had yet to discuss the future and even their relationship wasn't official. Everything had happened so fast and she was still reeling from the whirlwind of the past twenty four hours. Yesterday this time she didn't even know that Laku existed, and now she was envisioning a future with him.

The writer in her loved the daring recklessness and appreciated the intensity of it all. Laku had appeared from nowhere and claimed her heart. She had been in a state of nirvana since the second he walked into her life.

It was inspiring.

It was unbelievable.

It was real.

She was in love with him.

There was no use pretending otherwise.

Chapter 33

Jameer sobbed as he drove, salty tears trickling down the two-day stubble on his cheeks. He was driving aimlessly, the stench of his bodily waste pungent in the car. He was unable to smell himself, and he did not feel discomfort or disgust. He was in a labyrinth and all he could see were Laku's eyes staring at him, taunting him, scaring him at every turn. He could hear his voice too, oddly melodic and eerie.

If you ever contact Chasity again in any kind of way, I'm going to hunt you down and kill you.

It played over and over again, like a CD on repeat.

Serious.

Deadly.

Mocking.

"Leave me alone! You fucking demon!" Jameer screamed at the fiery red eyes, pressing down on the gas in exasperated fury.

He realized too late that the red eyes had given way to red lights.

There was a sickening crunch of metal as a bus heading in the direction of Old Hope Road hit Jameer's car at full force, sending it crashing into a wall several feet away.

He died instantly, his head severed from his body. The onlooker who was first on the scene, a young woman on her way back to campus – she was a dance student at the University of the Visual Arts which was close by – after walking to the gas station to purchase a phone card, threw up the three slices of pepperoni pizza that she had consumed for dinner a mere twenty-five minutes ago.

It was a gruesome scene. The young lady wondered as she wiped her mouth why the young man had run the red light and given away his life like that. Wherever he had been in a hurry to go could have waited. Now he would never reach.

A large crowd had now gathered.

She walked away somberly and headed towards the pedestrian entrance of the university as sirens neared.

She badly needed to brush her teeth.

It was the first time that she had witnessed some-one dying.

She hoped that it didn't give her nightmares.

Chasity walked confidently up to the podium to accept the award for Best Adult Creative Writing, the most coveted fiction award of the night. Usually she was nervous whenever she was the center of attention, especially sporting a new hairdo that was not her usual conservative style, but not tonight. And she knew that it was because of Laku. He truly brought out in the best in her. When they had entered the ballroom an hour ago, all eyes had been on them. People had really stared. And she couldn't blame them. She knew that they made a formidable couple. The energy that they gave off on top of how good they looked together was hard to ignore.

It had been a magical night so far. She didn't even mind that her parents were not there. She had not expected them to attend. Her father never approved of her pursuing a career in the Arts and her mother pretty much did anything her father said even if it meant not being supportive of her own daughter. Uncle Jeremiah, her mother's older brother who resided in England and who had done well for himself in business, had been the one to pay for her college tuition. He loved his only niece and had not hesitated when she turned to him. He recently had an operation on his back and was currently recuperating, and as such, was regrettably unable to make the trip to see her collect her award.

She got to the podium, accepted her award and a kiss on the cheek from Claude Chisolm, the President of the Jamaica Booksellers and Publishers Association. Some members of the audience applauded vigourously while others were more demure in their applause. She did not win the award for Best Fiction Cover. That went to M. Marie Renee, an author that Chasity had heard always had something bad to say about her, but this was the one that mattered. And she deserved it. *Life Interrupted* was without question the best fiction produced in Jamaica and perhaps the entire Caribbean region this year.

She had not prepared a speech as she had not intended to stay at the podium long if she won.

Holding her award, she went over to the microphone.

"Goodnight fellow writers, publishers, booksellers and book lovers. I'd like to thank God for bestowing on me this incredible talent, and I'd like to thank my publisher, Green Acres Publications, for believing in me. Mr. Green, you rock. I'd also like to give a special shout out to my loyal readers. Thanks for recognizing the good stuff when you see it."

The latter got a chuckle from some members of the audience. Chasity smiled and returned to her seat. The presentations continued. Laku was looking at her like he couldn't wait for them to get out of there.

He wasn't the only one.

She was wetter than a mermaid.

Chapter 34

"**H**ave you ever given any thought to how you are going die?" Chasity asked. They were snuggled up in bed in Laku's suite watching the movie Final Destination, the first and best installment in the five-film series.

"I'm already dead," Laku responded after a long pause.

Chasity looked up at him with a half-smile, wondering what he meant by that. By all accounts he led a very exciting and fulfilling life, and had everything to live for. That was the kind of statement that someone who had essentially given up on life and was merely going through the motions, just existing, would make.

"Why would you say that?"

Laku kissed her on her forehead.

"I'll explain one of these days," he told her.

She was not a nag so though she really wanted to know what he meant, she dropped it. He would explain when he was ready.

She touched her right breast and winced slightly. Laku gave the most brutal love bites. She didn't mind the pain when he was doing it while they made love. It somehow enhanced her pleasure, but afterwards it hurt like hell.

He had not told her about his confrontation with Jameer other than to say that the situation was taken care of and she didn't have to worry about it anymore. Apparently that should be enough for her. And it was. Though she couldn't help being curious about the details.

She was absolutely relieved that Jameer was out of her life without having a confrontation with him. Laku had spared her that and she was truly grateful. She hoped that Jameer would be ok as he moved on with his life but she didn't want to ever see or hear from him again. Whatever she had felt for him, which was never deep to begin with, had been slowly eroded by his metamorphosis into the asshole of the year.

She wanted someone to love her, not smother her. She cannot grow in the shade. And she also wanted to love that person in return. To truly experience giving and receiving love in its purest form. She was definitely in love with Laku, of that she had no doubts.

The question was, how did he really feel about her?

She knew that he cared about her. She knew that he respected her. She knew that he enjoyed her company. She knew that he enjoyed making love to her.

But did he love her?

She needed to know the answer.

And soon.

Her heart was anxiously waiting.

The movie ended and Laku started channel surfing. There were over a hundred to choose from. Chasity snuggled up closer to him and pulled the comforter up to her neck. She was getting sleepy. It had been a long, exciting day. She had finally started her new book. She had written the prologue and the first three chapters, she had gotten rid of Jameer, she had won an important literary award, and she had spent most of the day with a man that she was absolutely in love with. Surely it didn't get much better than that.

But then again, maybe it did. Laku had asked her to go back to Portland with him and stay at the villa until it was time for him to leave. She had told him yes. She had two freelance design jobs working on but it wouldn't be a problem working from Portland. All she needed was her laptop and internet service. Laku would provide the inspiration. Her creative juices were flowing. She was sure that she would complete the two jobs and make some serious headway with her novel, all while having a ball with Laku.

She was very excited about going to Portland to spend time alone with Laku. Portland was a very beautiful and laid back parish, and the villa where he was staying was touted as one of the Caribbean's most luxurious resorts. Perfect for a romantic getaway.

She refused to think about what was going to happen when he had to leave. No sense spoiling the fun they would have by worrying about that. She would cross that bridge when she got there.

She would spend the time immersing herself in the moment, basking in love, getting even closer to Laku and hopefully, learn a lot more about him. He was very mysterious to her. Strange even. A complex man. It would take more than nine days to peel away all his layers but it would be a start.

The thought of spending nine whole days in a plush villa with Laku filled her with goosebumps.

Sighing contentedly, she fell asleep with a smile.

Chapter 35

"Oh my God!" Chasity exclaimed. She was reading a local online newspaper on Laku's iPad while he ordered breakfast through room service, and saw the article about Jameer's gruesome death. She was absolutely stunned. In horror, she wondered for a fleeting second if Laku had had anything to do with his death.

I took care of it. He won't bother you anymore.

She frantically read the rest of the article. No, Laku had nothing to do it. She breathed a sigh of relief. Jameer ran a red light and got fatally punished by a bus. Based on the time it must have happened shortly after Laku picked her up at the complex to take her to the awards ceremony.

She said a quick prayer for his soul. She was really sorry to hear about his death. He had turned out to be a different person than she initially thought he was but she would never wish anything bad to happen to him.

Laku had gotten off of the phone and was looking at her.

"Jameer died in a car accident last night," Chasity told him.

"I'm sorry to hear that," Laku said. It was obvious that he was just being polite. "Do you still want to go to Portland?"

"Of course baby," Chasity answered quickly. "I mean ...I'm sorry that he's dead but he was out of my life. His death changes nothing."

I wonder if you'd feel the same way if you knew that I drove him to his death.

Laku nodded.

Not liking the stoic expression on his face, Chasity pushed the iPad aside and went over to him. She reached inside his robe. He was naked underneath. She cupped his testicles and ground them together gently. His shaft responded to her touch. It began to uncoil like an anaconda awakened from its slumber.

"Baby...I'm ok, really. Just got taken off guard by the news," she cooed, anxious to ease any discomfort he might be feeling, and hoping fervently that she was not being presumptuous that he might have felt uncomfortable because of her distraught reaction to Jameer's death.

Laku nodded again. "Its ok, I understand."

She squatted in front of him and ran her tongue along the considerable length of his shaft. Generally, she did not fancy giving fellatio, but there was no part on Laku's body that she didn't enjoy pleasing. He was just so sexy and desirable. And she loved him.

She held his buttocks as she took him inside her mouth slowly, gasping and drooling when he was almost all the way in. He rocked gently in her mouth as she wrapped her tongue around his member and sucked him languidly.

She hoped she could bring him to climax before the food arrived.

She was certainly going to try.

"Baby I need to go and get my stuff. Its almost check out time," Chasity said after breakfast, which she had enjoyed while Laku watched her eat. She just couldn't understand it. Laku was never hungry. When she asked him about it all he would say was that he had unusual eating habits. It was now 11:15 a.m. and from her experience, most hotels required guests to check out by midday, some even as early as 11:30.

"Take the truck and go get your things," Laku told her. "We won't be leaving until about 6:30."

"Ok...well why don't we just check out and then stay at my apartment until we're ready to leave. That way you won't have to pay for another day."

Laku smiled indulgently. "I'll see your apartment another time. I have a rare skin condition. I can't be in the sun."

Chasity looked at him in bewilderment.

"Are you serious?"

"As a heart attack."

Chasity shook her head. Wow. That placed a lot of limitations on some of the things that she had planned to do in Portland. She wanted to take Laku to some of the tourist attractions such as the world famous Blue Lagoon and go rafting on the Rio Grande. Such things could not be done at night. But then again, it rained often in Portland and it was a very cool parish so just maybe he would be able to venture out. She wasn't too perturbed though, they would still have a great time regardless.

"Ok, I'll go home and get my things, see you in a bit."

She kissed him and got up to get dressed. She slipped on her dress that she had worn to the ceremony, put on her heels and went to the bathroom to comb her hair.

Six minutes later she was in the rented Mercedes SUV heading out of the hotel's expansive parking lot. She loved the truck. It was rugged, masculine and completely luxurious.

She thought about Laku on the short drive home.

He was such a very strange and intriguing man.

She had an uncanny feeling that there were a lot of surprises to come.

She hoped that she would be able to handle them.

Laku, still wearing his robe, thought about Chasity as he listened to Green Day on his iPod. He was pleased that she was so excited about going to Portland with him. He was looking forward to it as well. The Palms was a place for lovers. Now he would be able to truly enjoy the experience.

Nine days of fun and bliss.

And then what?

He was no closer to the answer though the question was never far from his mind.

He was trying to keep his emotions in check and not get too deeply involved with Chasity despite the fact that it was clear to him that the more he spent time with her; the more he would be fighting a losing battle. He had come to Jamaica for fun and adventure. Blood and sex in an exotic location that he had never been to before. He had enjoyed some great sex and would be having lots more but he was yet to have some blood. That was something he would have to rectify soon as he would not leave without having a taste of island blood. That would be a travesty. It would be a bit tricky with Chasity there with him but he would figure something out.

Love.

He didn't come to Jamaica for love.

Apparently love didn't care.

He was headed down a road that had bittersweet memories.

And there was no turning back.

Chapter 36

"**I**s our French guest back as yet?" Toi asked Randy, one of the bell boys who worked on the night shift.

"No, I haven't seen him," Randy answered with a smirk. It was the biggest gossip around the hotel amongst the bell boys and cleaning staff that Toi, who acted as though her legs were glued together, had slept with the French man the same night he checked in. She was trying to act like it was a casual question but he wasn't fooled. He could see the anxiety in her eyes.

"Ok, thanks," Toi said, and walked away.

Randy watched her head to her office, her voluptuous ass hypnotizing him as it bounced sexily in the close confines of her fitted black slacks. He shook his head wistfully. Guess he had to be handsome and rich to get a piece of that. He had been surprised when his close friend Gary, who worked on the day shift, called to tell him that he saw Toi leaving the guest's villa about two hours after she had gotten off work and was supposed to have gone home.

Randy had found it hard to believe that Toi had not only given up the goods to a stranger, but had risked her job like that. She was fortunate that despite the fact that she wouldn't give any of them the time of day, she had a nice personality and didn't treat them like most of the other managers did.

Her secret was safe with them.

Laku drove in after briefly speaking with the security guard at the gate. He parked in the courtyard-looking parking lot which was designated for the three villas in this section of the lush property.

"Welcome to paradise," he said, smiling at Chasity.

She released her seatbelt and leaned over until her face was inches away from his.

"I've been in paradise from the moment you entered my life…"

Laku looked deep into her eyes. They were a kaleidoscope of emotions. Love. Affection. Admiration. Lust. Fear. Desire. Need. The latter jarred him. She needed him. That touched him deeply. He read her mind. Her love was real, pure. Virginal in its expression. No one had ever before been the object of her affection so deeply. She feared not being able to make him understand just how much she was in love with him before he went back to France. She feared what was going to happen when it was time for him to go back. She was out on an emotional limb and she was terrified of falling.

He wished that he could soothe her fears but he had his own grappling with. He wanted to release his burden and show himself to her, let her truly see just what she was in love with. But he feared her rejection. He feared that her love for him would be corrupted by the insanity of realizing that the man she was in so in love with was not a man, but a vampire.

She would recoil, her face a mask of incredulity and disgust, her brain feeling like it was going to explode as it struggled to come to terms with fiction becoming fact, and fantasy merging into reality. The rich, handsome, cultured, sophisticated lothario that had swept her off her feet was a soulless monster that was at the top of the food chain. Could her love for him withstand that? He dreaded the answer.

He had long come to terms with himself. He was at peace. But to ask someone to accept it and also to eventually become the same so that they could coexist forever was too much. His love for Franciska had been strong enough. It had fought through the incredulity of it all, and had been willing to make the ultimate sacrifice.

But though he knew just how much Chasity loved him, he didn't know if it was deep enough, strong enough, to withstand a test of such magnitude. Only a very special love could. And very few people experienced that kind of love in their lifetime.

He was very powerful and had a number of special skills.

But not even he could predict the future.

He would have to find out the old fashioned way like a mere mortal.

He kissed her gently.

"Let's go inside."

They climbed out of the SUV and Laku retrieved his two bags and as well as the two that Chasity had brought.

"Let me help you baby," Chasity offered.

"I can manage," Laku told her, toting the four bags like they were empty. Chasity could only smile. He was so strong. She walked behind him along the softly lit, palm-tree lined stone path. They got to the gate of the villa, a high wooden gate that was covered with foliage, which prevented anyone from seeing the villa from the outside.

"Wow, this is really nice," Chasity commented. The villa was completely private. You could run around in the front yard naked. No one would see you. High walls, completely covered with foliage and buffered by plants and trees, cloaked the villa in privacy.

She could hear water. Instead of going inside with Laku, she went around to the back of the villa. She stood and looked in awe. Thirty feet away was one of the prettiest beaches that Chasity had ever laid eyes upon.

The calm moon-kissed water looked very inviting. Slipping off her sandals, and carrying them in her hand, she walked out to the beach as if hypnotized, and marveled as the powder-like soft white sand caressed her bare feet. The cool breeze made her nipples press forcefully against her ribbed tank top.

She gasped in fright as she felt Laku's lips on the back of her neck. He always moved so stealthily. Her heart galloped and her body warmed instantly.

"Baby...you're going to give me a heart attack one of these days..." she murmured, dropping her sandals and reaching over with her free hand to caress his cheek.

She turned around and laughed out loud in surprise. Laku was naked and had a huge beach towel in his hand. Her eyes glazed over with lust. She was about to go skinny dipping for the first time. She was very excited. Her juices were already flowing.

"Someone seems to be a tad bit overdressed..." Laku said softly. He placed the towel on the sand, and then removed her tank top, bra, shorts and underwear, dropping them on top of the towel.

He then turned her back around and bent her over,

making her place her hands on the sand. She shivered in ecstasy when his cold tongue invaded her pussy from behind.

"Oh baby…oh my God…mmmm…that feels so good…"

Laku fucked her with his tongue like it was battery operated. It massaged her sugar walls as it went in and out, going impossibly deep inside her hot core, making her grip fistfuls of sand and howl at the moon like a wild animal.

Her unexpected vacation had gotten off to an excellent start.

Chapter 37

Toi paced her office like a bitch in heat. Randy had just told her that the French guest had returned. The Mercedes SUV was in the parking lot. She had thanked him and closed the office door. Her body had transformed the minute that she heard the news. It started to immediately relive the sensuous moments that she had shared with him. She just couldn't understand the effect that this man had on her. She was so desperate to see him that she didn't know what to do with herself.

She checked the time. It was now 8:30 p.m. She would give him another hour before giving him a call under the pretext of checking if he was ok and if he needed anything. Just the thought of hearing his voice gave her goose bumps. She felt like a love-struck, lust-filled teenager.

Last night during sex with Merrick, her live-in boyfriend, she had thought of Laku the entire time, wishing that he was the one inside her, filling her up, making her climax until she was exhausted. It was unfair to compare them, but she couldn't help it. Merrick paled in comparison to Laku in every single way. She sighed wistfully. Merrick was a good man and he loved her. He didn't deserve this but it was like Laku had her under a spell. She knew that she needed to get herself together before she got herself in trouble with her employer and with her boyfriend.

But she had to have Laku even one more time.

She simply had to.

Sex like that could not be experienced only once.

Chasity's stomach rumbled in an unfeminine manner. She smiled at Laku, wondering if he had heard it. The twinkle in his mesmerizing red eyes gave her the answer. They were at Forest Fare, a tree top restaurant that you had to see to believe. Lushly exquisite, the one of a kind restaurant boasted a forest-to-ocean view that would wow even the most jaded traveler.

The night was starry and cool, providing the perfect complement to the heavenly ambiance of the restaurant. It was spacious, and Laku and Chasity were seated on the right side, several tables away from the nearest guests, two Caucasian couples who were having a grand time, if their laughter-filled conversation was anything to go by.

Chasity looked at Laku. She just couldn't get over how beautiful he was for a man. She couldn't think of a single movie star that came even close to him in the looks department. He was truly blessed. In so many ways. She winced slightly as she adjusted herself on the comfortable chair. Laku had put a serious hurting on her down by the beach.

She was so exhausted and sore when he was through with her that he had to throw her over his shoulder and take her inside the villa. Laku had invented sex. There could be no other explanation for his unparalleled sexual prowess.

The waiter arrived with their order. Chasity had ordered duck confit Panini with fig moustarda and curried chicken salad wrapped in moist, chewy Indian paratha bread. As usual, Laku was not eating. Chasity just couldn't understand how he could have a body like that and be so strong when he hardly ever ate. But she had met him this way, and he seemed fine with his 'unusual eating habits' as he had put it, so it served no purpose to keep asking him about it.

Laku sipped his wine and smiled as he watched Chasity eat. He loved when a woman enjoyed food, and wasn't afraid to eat healthy portions. As long as it didn't show in unflattering places.

"Good?"

Chasity swallowed a mouthful before responding.

"Absolutely delicious," she responded, wondering if he would taste it. No such luck. He merely took another sip of his wine.

"Christmas is my favourite time of the year," Chasity commented. She was excited about spending it with Laku.

Laku looked over at the ocean for a few moments before responding.

"This time of year holds bad memories for me. My parents died in a car accident around this time three years ago."

"Oh my God, I'm so sorry baby. I can only imagine how painful that was for you." She reached over and touched his hand gently. Both her parents were still alive and though her relationship with them was strained, at least they were alive.

"It was very painful. I absorb pain the same as I do pleasure. A very intense way to live but I would have it no other way. Besides, it's good for my art."

He gave her a smile and she smiled back, relieved that she had not changed the mood by inadvertently jarring that dreadful memory.

Chasity suddenly felt nervous. She wanted to tell him that she loved him but was afraid of what he would say, or think. There was no question that some-thing special and rare was occurring between them, at least in her eyes, but it was entirely possible that Laku simply liked her a lot and was just having a good time, enjoying her company until it was time to go home.

She didn't even know if he had a woman back in France. He did not wear a wedding ring but that didn't mean he wasn't married. A man like Laku was a prize catch. It was highly unlikely that he didn't have someone special in his life.

She had never been this emotionally scared in her life. She felt like she was about to have a panic attack. To be so deeply in love with someone with so much uncertainty and unknown variables in the mix was as crazy as a soup sandwich. But that was love for you. A pure, unsolicited emotion that was contemptuous of reason and logic.

She decided to jump off the cliff.

"I love you."

Laku was looking at her intently, but she couldn't read his expression. She continued her free fall.

"I don't know if you want my heart, but it's yours. I don't know how we got here – how I got here – but it is what it is. I'm totally in love with you."

Laku looked at her steadily as he read her mind. She had taken a leap of faith and was now frozen in mid-air, hoping that he would catch her, mortified that he might let her fall, her heart smashed to pieces, jagged and uneven like broken glass.

Love. Love had an evil twin. Ying and yang. It could make you strong, and it could also make you very weak. It could give you the sweetest pleasure known to man, and it could also make you feel excruciating pain.

Laku's silence was unnerving. It was not the reaction that Chasity was hoping for. He didn't want her. Her declaration had taken the fun out of it for him. It was going to push him away. She had made a fool of herself. Tears sprang forth, despite her best efforts to keep them at bay. Her lip-gloss coated lips trembled as she struggled to contain herself.

Laku moved so fast she didn't even realize that he had until she felt his lips against hers. It was a gentle kiss. A reassuring kiss. He then kissed her tear-stained cheeks, her eyes, and her forehead.

"I love you too, Chasity."

She erupted in sobs.

They were tears of relief.

Tears of joy.

Was there anything in the world quite like the person that you love, loving you back? She didn't think so. It was a feeling like no other.

"Would you do anything for love?" Laku asked quietly.

Instinctively, Chasity knew that it wasn't a casual question. Would she do *anything* for love? She looked into Laku's eyes. They were burning with even more intensity than usual. She touched his face. This was it for her. In a few short days she had experienced a level of happiness that was surreal. There was no way on earth that she could feel for someone else what she felt for the incredible man sitting across from her. This was the only man for her. Yes, she would do anything for him, for love.

"Yes...yes I would."

Laku knew that she had answered truthfully but just because she believed it didn't make it so.

"We're going to put that to the test real soon."

He looked so serious that Chasity had a hollow feeling in her stomach.

She wondered what the test would be.

Well whatever it was, she had to pass it.

That was the bottom line.

She had unexpectedly found true love.

She was not going to lose it.

Chapter 38

Toi frowned and hung up the phone. That was her second call to Laku's villa without an answer. Perhaps he was sleeping. But it was early. It was only 10 p.m. and he had seemed to be a very nocturnal type of person. It was highly unlikely that he had already gone to bed. She decided to go over there. She simply had to see him. It was a quiet night, and Charlene, the receptionist, should be able to handle anything that might arise until she got back.

She headed out of her office and closed the door.

"Charlene, I'll be back in a few. If you need me call me on my mobile," she said as she breezed through the lobby.

Charlene nodded and went back to updating her Facebook status.

She walked briskly towards the villa, her heart pounding with nervous excitement. She passed Randy on the way. He smiled at her knowingly but didn't comment. She was almost at the gate to Laku's villa when he arrived from the direction of the restaurant. Her mood changed drastically when she realized that he was not alone.

He looked over at her. His eyes were luminous like two fireflies in the low light.

"Hello Toi," he said politely. "This is Chasity. Chasity meet Toi, she's the night shift manager of the property."

"Hi, nice to meet you," Chasity said. She did not attempt to shake her hand. She was getting a hostile vibe from the young lady. Instinctively, she knew that it had something to do with Laku. Perhaps she liked him and was surprised to see him with a woman seeing as he had checked into the villa alone when he first arrived.

Toi nodded stiffly, as she tried to keep her composure. Who the hell was this bitch? She wished that she could slap the taste out of her mouth. She was holding on to Laku's arm possessively like he belonged to her. Chasity. What kind of name was that anyway?

"How was your trip?" Toi asked, ignoring Chasity.

"It was great. I'll see you around." He then opened the gate and allowed Chasity to go in, and closed it behind them.

Toi was still standing there. She was trembling with rage. She didn't know what she had expected, but she felt really embarrassed at the way in which he had casually dismissed her like he didn't have intimate knowledge of her body. Like they hadn't shared an amazing experience. She felt used. Stupid. Embarrassed. She meant nothing to him. Just some chick he had fucked on his first night on the island. Now it was on to the next one.

And that bitch. She thought she was cute. Holding on to Laku's arm possessively and smirking like she had won the lottery.

She turned and walked back slowly to the hotel administration building.

She felt lower than the belly of an ant.

There was an air of expectancy as they settled down in the living room area. Laku sat on the love seat and Chasity sat on the plush rug in front of it. She looked up at him. She was going to make a light joke about Toi liking him and being jealous of her but she sensed that now wasn't the time for jokes. Laku seemed to have something important to say to her, but was reluctant to say it. It was making her uneasy. It amazed her how in tune she was to his emotions in such a short space of time.

"I didn't plan to address this issue until it was time for me to leave. Matter of fact, I wasn't sure if I was even going to. I was leaving my options open and leaving without dealing with it was one of the two options. But you have forced my hand. You have bravely thrown caution to the wind and told me how you feel about me and what you want. I would be a coward not to do the same."

Chasity listened keenly and anxiously. She was deathly afraid of where this was going. Her mind tortured her with the possibilities. He was married. That was it. He was going to tell her that he had a wife back home. She had fallen madly in love with a man that wasn't available. Destiny was a menstruating bitch. To give someone a taste of true happiness and to quickly snatch it away was beyond cruel.

"So I told you. Now we have both acknowledged the fact that this is not a casual fling. It's a destined alignment of two compatible souls. An alignment that will change our lives forever...if we continue along this path."

Chasity felt a sudden urge to pee. But she didn't dare move.

"I am what you think I am. I am the person you fell in love with. And I am not. There is more to me Chasity. Much more. And when I reveal this to you, it will be extremely difficult for your brain to process it. And you will understand what I meant when I said that this will prove if you will do anything for love."

He stood and held out his hand.

"Come with me."

Chasity rose unsteadily and took his hand.

She felt confused, anxious and afraid.

Her heart couldn't take the suspense.

Laku led her to the bathroom.

Chapter 39

Laku stopped by the bathroom door and gestured for her to go in. Chasity wondered if he could hear her heart beating. It sounded really loud to her ears. She walked in slowly and turned to face him. He looked solemn, afraid even. It was the first time since she met him that she had seen a chink in his perfect armour. It humanized him, and somehow made him even more perfect in her eyes.

He was afraid of losing her. He loved her that much. Her heart, despite its terrified state, smiled in the face of its terror. She wanted to hug him and kiss him, and convince him that he had nothing to fear. That there was nothing on earth that could make her stop loving him, stop wanting to be with him. But she did none of those things. The only thing that would convince Laku was to listen to what he had to tell her, and then show him that the revelation had changed nothing.

"You have noticed some strange things about me," he began, looking at her intensely as he spoke. "My body temperature is always cold. You have never seen me eat. You have never seen me sleep. I am very strong. I sometimes move so quickly that it happens before you even realize it."

He paused, allowing her to relive the memory of a time that she had noticed each of these things. He watched as she frowned, deep in thought, as memories of the past couple of days played like a slide show.

"I seem to always know what you're thinking. I have incredible stamina. I can make love to you all night. My voice is melodic, seductive. Everything about me pulls you in, like a moth to a flame."

Chasity was trembling now. What did all of this mean? Relief that it didn't appear that he was married was temporary. It lasted only for a fleeting second. It was immediately replaced by a new anxiety. Was he like that because he was on some type of drug? Several different drugs? That wasn't so bad. He could get help, go to rehab. She would be there for him every step of the way. But it didn't seem like a plausible explanation. Laku simply did not seem like the kind of man to use drugs. And what drug in the world had those kinds of effects on a human being? None that she had ever heard of, that was for sure.

"Chasity..."

"Yes baby..." Her voice was a croak. It sounded unfamiliar to her ears.

"Turn and face the mirror."

Bewildered, and feeling like her heart was clanging against her chest, Chasity slowly turned until she was facing the mirror.

Her reflection stunned her. If the eyes were indeed mirrors to the soul, hers was a messy room of turmoil, fear and anxiety. Every emotion that she was feeling was showing on her face.

Laku was now standing behind her.

His cold hands were on her shoulders.

It took several seconds, but her brain finally processed the fact that she could not his reflection in the mirror.

"B-b-b-baby..." she stuttered as she placed her hands on top of his. Yes, his hands were there on her shoulder. She turned her head to look at him. Yes, he was standing there. She turned back around to look in the mirror. Only her confused and terrified eyes stared back at her, asking the same question she was asking. What in the world was going on?

She began to tremble mightily. She felt dizzy, nauseous. Her chest tightened and she felt a burning sensation in her face. Her breathing became constricted and she felt like she was choking. She swore that she was going to die.

Laku lifted her in his arms and took her to the bedroom. He placed her in the middle of the bed gently and in a flash, was in the kitchen pouring a glass of water. He took it back to her and made her sit up. He spoke soothingly to her and the panic attack subsided as quickly as it had appeared. He held the glass of water to her lips. She drank every drop.

She had now stopped shaking completely and her breathing had returned to normal, but her heart was still beating incredibly fast and she was still in a state of confusion. She looked at him.

"You had a panic attack," Laku told her.

Chasity had heard about panic attacks but had no idea that they were that intense and horrible. She hoped that she never experienced one again. Thank God Laku had known exactly what to do.

"Laku...who – what are you?" she asked softly.

Laku returned her gaze. Her mind was covered with a thick fog of confusion. She was struggling to comprehend just what was really going on. There was no turning back now. He had already gone halfway and they were now at the critical juncture. Either it would all end here, or it would be the start of a new beginning.

"I'm a vampire."

Time stopped.

What Laku was saying was impossible. Vampires did not exist. They were not real. This was not a TV show, a movie or a novel. This was reality. And yet she knew without a doubt that he spoke the truth.

Laku read her mind. It was like listening to several people talking at the same time. He didn't find what he was looking for. At least not yet. She wasn't yet repulsed by him, she wasn't afraid, but perhaps that was due to the fact that what he told her had yet to really sink in. Her brain was rejecting the preposterousness of his statement.

"I'm going to tell you everything. Don't speak until I'm through. Just listen."

Chasity nodded numbly.

Laku began, starting with the fateful night that he met Franciska. He completely opened up his world to Chasity and for the next hour, Chasity listened to the most incredible story that she had ever heard, while going through more emotions than ten menstruating women.

It had not been necessary for Laku to tell her not to speak.

She couldn't even if she wanted to.

She was speechless.

Chapter 40

Chasity was shivering in the cold night air. She barely noticed as she walked along the incredibly beautiful, deserted beach. After listening to Laku's story, she had laid there, dazed and shell-shocked for several minutes. Or it could have been seconds or even hours. She had no idea. Her concept of time was non-existent at the moment. Hell, her concept of life as she knew it had just been shattered. There was an alternate reality out there. Completely alien to what she knew. Fantasy existing within the context of reality. She had left the villa without speaking, and headed out to the beach. Laku had not followed.

What Laku had shared with her was too incredible. Too unbelievable. If it were a manuscript no publisher would touch it and if it were a screenplay no producer would accept it. But she was neither a publisher nor a producer. She was the woman that had fallen deeply in love with him. And she either had to accept it or run like the wind. Run away from the fascinating insanity of it all. But she knew that the latter was not an option. She had gotten a taste of what true love was really like, had gotten a preview of what real happiness felt like, and there was no way that she could walk away from it. Her experiences over the past couple of days, culminating in the nuclear bomb that Laku dropped tonight, had made her a different person.

A wise man once said that every true artist was crazy because imagination and insanity were first cousins. She had always been rather quirky and out there mentally, but after learning that the man she loved was a vampire who fed on human blood, which he painfully extracted, killing them in the process, didn't stop her from loving and wanting to be with him, she had to wonder if imagination and insanity weren't in fact, identical twins.

She looked up at the starry sky. It was a beautiful, chaotic, eventful night. One that would forever be etched in her memory. Laku had laid all his cards on the table. If she decided to accept him for who he was, and stay with him, she would one day have to become like him so that they could truly be together.

It wouldn't do for her to have a handsome virile partner who would look that way forever while she was aging and subject to mortality. No, she couldn't do this half-way. But there was time. Laku wasn't rushing her. All he wanted was to know that she would be with him. By her reckoning, she had at least two years before taking that final step. She would be twenty-six in two years. Laku was twenty-five when he became a vampire. Though depending on how things panned out, she might even do it earlier.

France. That would be her new home. Living in luxury in a secluded mansion with Laku. Free to do as they wished, whenever they wished. She got goose bumps as she thought about how her new experiences would shape her writing. Laku had told her that he had done his best work when he became a vampire. Perhaps it would be that way for her. She had to learn the French language. Well enough to be able to write a book in French. That would be awesome.

There wasn't much that she would be leaving behind when it was time to move away. For the first year they could visit each other while she tied up loose ends here such as fulfilling her obligations to her publisher by finishing up *Shackles* and promoting it. She wouldn't miss her parents greatly; she hardly saw them as it was. She didn't have many close friends, and her best friend, Sabrina, whom she had yet to tell about Laku – she was going to have a fit at the developments – lived in Florida. She would not be able to tell Sabrina everything. There was no way that she would even believe or understand. And revealing one's self was forbidden. Chasity now considered herself one of the chosen few. Enlightened and special.

She had made her decision.

And she had been right.

She would indeed do anything for love.

She turned around and walked back towards the villa, her delicate feet sinking into the soft white sand.

She could see Laku's silhouette on the back patio.

He was waiting for her.

She ran to him.

Epilogue

*L*aku, dressed in all black, waited impatiently for Chasity to clear customs. He was in the arrival area at the Paris-Charles de Gaulle Airport to pick up Chasity. It had been eighteen months since that night at the villa in Jamaica, when he told Chasity everything. Since that time, he had been back to Jamaica three times, and Chasity had been to France twice. This time, her trip would be permanent.

He had proposed to her at midnight, on the last day of her trip the last time she came to Paris, on the Pont Alexandre 111, the most beautiful, opulently decorated bridge in the city. She had cried, whispering yes over and over again through her joyous tears.

It still to this day amazed Laku how fate had brought them together, and he was eternally grateful that Chasity had, despite the fact that her life would have been irrevocably changed forever, embraced her fate.

She enriched his existence in a way that he hadn't thought possible. He loved her with every fiber in his being. They would have their challenges, especially when it was time to change her. But she would have him by her side to help with the transition every step of the way. She would not have to figure everything out on her own, the way he had. The transition would not be seamless, but it would be manageable.

Eternity had a nice ring to it now that he had someone that he loved to share it with.

He loved Chasity so much that he wondered if eternity would be enough.

Chasity smiled sweetly when the custom's officer complimented her on her French as he stamped her Jamaican passport. She had worked hard at learning it the right way, and between Laku, a private tutor, and Rosetta Stone, she had done a tremendous job and now was practically fluent.

It had been a hell of a journey to get to this point but the real journey was just now beginning. She was about to start her new life with Laku, leaving everything and everyone behind. She was at peace with herself, with her choice, with where her life was about to go. She was in such a constant state of euphoria that she sometimes had nightmares that something would happen that would rob her of her happiness.

She went to see her parents at their home in Ocho Rios to tell them goodbye. It had been brief and awkward. She knew deep down that she would never see them again. The six month old child in her belly would never know his grandparents. And with Laku's parents dead, all he would have were his parents. His undead, vampire parents. Chasity and Laku had, after much deliberation, decided to have a child. They had to do it before Chasity was changed as it would be impossible for her to get pregnant once she became a vampire.

The child, who they were going to name Anpu, in honour of Laku's Egyptian heritage, and which meant 'royal child', was going to be born half-human, half-vampire. A natural day-walker with supernatural powers. He would be a king among men. And with two extremely creative and talented parents, Chasity could only imagine how talented Anpu was going to be. It had been a very good pregnancy. She rarely had morning sickness, or mood swings and was glowing with joy and contentment. Anpu was going to be a big baby. At six months he made his mother's stomach look like she was going to be having twins.

"Merci, ont une bonne nuit," Chasity said, as she walked away from the window. She was travelling very light. Anything of consequence that she needed had already been air freighted ahead.

Her heart pounded as she approached the exit. It was like this every time that she was about to see him. His son seemed to sense his presence too. He had started to move.

There was so much to look forward to.

Anpu's birth and development. Her transformation into a vampire and the changes that would come with that. Life as an unconventional family.

Eternal bliss with the man she loved.

She was blessed.

Fate had given her a choice.

And she had chosen happiness.

She smiled broadly when her choice came into view.

About the Author

K. Sean Harris is a national best-selling author, and the Caribbean's most exciting and prolific author of adult contemporary fiction. He has written twelve successful books over the past six years. For more information on the talented word-smith, visit his official website www.kseanharris.com.